*"THE HIGHW... ... ...
AT ALL! HE—ER SHE...*

"Bring the wench here," ordered the Duke.

The girl flushed deeply as the Duke's cold, green eyes stripped her from top to toe, remarking the multi-patched coat with torn pocket, the tattered remnants crying out to be a waistcoat, kneebreeches minus knees, crudely shod, stockingless feet, and thread-bare shirt, beneath which he perceived the voluptuous fullness of a well-matured female form. Even had she not been preoccupied with her recent trouble, she would never have discerned her effect upon him. It was not the incomparable beauty of her which played havoc with the Duke's self-control, but something more profound— capable of rousing his long-dormant passion.

His lips curled into the sardonic sneer he invariably held at the ready, and a malicious look of self-satisfaction overspread his countenance.

"Well . . .," he purred, like a cat having run a fat juicy mouse to earth. " 'Twould seem Dame Fortune has at last smiled my way."

THE
PRICE OF
VENGEANCE

by Freda Michel

A FAWCETT CREST BOOK

Fawcett Publications, Inc., Greenwich, Connecticut

THE PRICE OF VENGEANCE

THIS BOOK CONTAINS THE COMPLETE TEXT OF
THE ORIGINAL HARDCOVER EDITION.

A Fawcett Crest Book reprinted by arrangement with Robert
Hale & Company.

ISBN 0-449-23211-5

Printed in the United States of America

10 9 8 7 6 5 4 3 2 1

THE
PRICE OF
VENGEANCE

1

A startled rabbit scurried to its burrow as a coach suddenly swung into view from behind a thicket, on a particularly deserted stretch of the London-to-Bath road betwixt Marlborough and Chippenham. The sturdy coachman (although well accustomed to the dangers lurking on the English roads in the mid-eighteenth century) cast a furtive glance all around before hastily crossing himself, and hunching his heavy becaped shoulders against the eerie moonlit night, muttered something unintelligible to his liveried companion as he whipped the perfectly matched team into further action.

However, if those atop of the vehicle seemed visibly nervous, those inside were evidently not, as their animated conversation penetrated the elaborately crested panels to be borne out into the night—dominated by an overexcited, decidedly female voice.

"It was wonderful! Wonderful!" cried the Lady Isabella Marie Louise Claremont, eagerly, for the twentieth time in the last two miles, to her audience of three fashionable gentlemen. "I never dreamed anything could be so . . ."

"Wonderful," obliged the most extravagantly attired of the three, with unmistakable cynicism.

"Yes, Gideon—wonderful!" approved his seventeen-year-old sister, gaily clapping her soft white hands. "I have never enjoyed myself quite so much in all my life! The Louvre! The Tuileries! The balls! The gowns! The jewels!

7

Just fancy, good sirs, I saw a ruby as big as a patch-box!" This met with apposite expressions of admiration by the gentlemen, and she resumed. "And there were peacocks in dozens, of a variety of hues—just like the ladies of the court—oh, the ladies!—"

"And the gentlemen," cut in her brother, disdainfully.

"Chandeliers like summer-houses!" she went on, undeterred. "And the music!—undoubtedly, gentlemen, King Louis has the best Court musicians in the whole world! And the courtiers!—so dainty that I vow their feet did not touch the floor!"

"Indeed, m' lady!" gasped Viscount Sevington, the taller and handsomer of the two remaining gentlemen, astonishment registering in his bright blue eyes, as if he had not already seen and heard all for himself.

"Oh, my lord!" she exclaimed ardently, her round pretty face flushed with excitement. "How I wish you could have been there."

"You wish it no more fervently than I," he responded, unexpectedly serious, a flame of passion flaring in his eyes.

The Lady Isabella flushed even deeper—but not with excitement—and swiftly averted her face from his steady gaze, though mindful to display her best profile to advantage.

"Er—did you visit Versailles, your ladyship?" piped up the Honourable Rowland Chalmers—the remaining gentleman, deeming it time he made himself heard.

"But of course, sir!—Gideon took me himself!" she responded, tossing her glossy brown ringlets. "And I was presented to King Louis and Queen Maria! They asked how long I was to stay—I swear, I was completely overwhelmed!—was I not, Gideon?"

"Quite, m' dear," sighed her brother with ennui, his long pallid fingers seeking diversion with his diamond-set eye-glass.

"You perhaps forget, Lady Isabella," reproved the fair-haired viscount kindly. "Gideon has spent half his life in France and so considers these wonders little more than commonplace." He smiled across at his most intimate friend—who honoured him with a weak inclination of his head.

And so, while my lady chattered on—as she had done ever since her return from France three days ago—her brother, namely, Gideon Cornelius Alexander Claremont, sixth Duke of Delvray, and head of one of the oldest and richest families in the land, reclined at his ease with his long superbly-moulded legs propped upon the opposite seat. His Grace looked about to expire of boredom at any moment, finding little consolation in the knowledge that his array—from silver-laced cocked hat perched jauntily upon raven-black locks, to diamond buckled shoes—was in the height of fashion. Or that the emerald nestling in the snowy Mechlin lace beneath his smooth determined chin was the largest in Christendom! However, it may have been because of the aquiline tendency of his nose, or the cynical curl of his thin-lipped mouth, or even the offensive penetration of his green eyes, that he remained utterly impervious to the unanimous acclaim by Society's distaff side, that he was disturbingly handsome and the wildest catch on the marriage mart.

But his face—handsome or no—remained bored-to-death, he finding nothing of interest in his sister's interminable high-pitched prattle which he had already endured a full six weeks.

"—and the Galerie des Glaces was a veritable paradise,

like heaven itself!—was it not, Gideon?" persisted she.

"Alas, 'Bella! There you have the advantage of me," he drawled, indolently. "The Celestial Heights is one place I have yet to see."

Lady Isabella emitted a peal of laughter. "I meant, like I imagine it to be. It reminded me also of the Crystal Salon at Claremont Park."

"Which his French Majesty has obviously sought to emulate," he parried, sober-faced, evoking another chuckle.

"Did you chance to meet any other illustrious personages, my lady?" broke in Rowland at this point, rubicund face agog, which contrasted vividly with the whiteness of his liberally powdered Ramillies wig.

"More than I could possibly recall, Mr. Chalmers," she cried eagerly, her voice suddenly dropping to a confidential whisper. "I saw even the infamous Pompadour—"

"Y-You what?" ejaculated the Viscount, aghast, whilst Rowland strove to recover his countenance. "S-Surely even Gideon—"

"No! No, my lord!" my lady endeavoured to reassure the horrified Viscount. "I merely saw her at a distance, nothing more."

"Hum! A great distance, I trust," mumbled the other, flashing the Duke a questioning glance, which availed him nought, as usual.

"My lady," Rowland ventured to change the inflammatory topic. "Did you visit the Gardens—and the Orangery? I am told they are truly admirable."

Her huge brown eyes gleamed acknowledgment. "And you are not deceived, sir," she accorded, emphasizing the fact with a tap on his broadcloth sleeve with her fan of painted vellum. "I declare it the most admirable orangery

I have ever seen—and the Gardens!"—she seemed to faint away completely. "They quite take one's breath away—do they not, Gideon?"

The Duke heaved yet another sigh. "If you say so, m' dear."

"As for the Palace itself," she extolled in raptures. "Indeed, Mr. Chalmers, you simply must escort your Mrs. Chalmers hence next season—for mere words cannot do it justice. It is far, far too grand—is it not, brother dear?"

"Prostrating," he corroborated, torpidly.

This did not have the daunting effect intended, for she then launched into a much embellished account of the Palace, with gusto.

"And how did Gideon pass the time?" queried the Viscount at the end of her harangue, blind to the hornets' nest he was rousing.

"Oh, in the usual way!" retorted my lady, throwing her brother a disparaging look. "Drinking, gaming, and consorting with those . . . those . . . unmentionable women!" She spat out the words, then shuddered, as if fearing some contamination.

"Women of easy virtue, is the polite term, 'Bella, so I believe," supplied his Grace, obligingly.

Viscount Sevington was not amused. 'Would Gideon never change?' he queried inwardly, realising how little he yet knew him, although they had been close friends since boyhood—aware that he had not fully recovered from the wound he had received from a certain beautiful and treacherous woman, which no manner of salve could heal—a wound to his heart. The deep reverent love he had borne her had died a tortuous death, to be replaced by a cold contempt for anything connected—however remotely —with that tender passion. Conducting his sordid life in the very presence of his sister proved just how callous he had become. Fervently, the Viscount hoped that one day soon his friend would find a new enduring love which would revolutionise his way of life, transporting him from the depths of his wickedness to the ethereal heights of everlasting happiness . . . in truth, a love as he himself had found.

The object of his heart broke in upon his reveries with her tinkling laughter, and raising his eyes to her delightful face, he sat watching her intently, wondering if she would ever acknowledge him as anything more than her brother's friend.

"Did you visit anywhere else, Gideon?" probed Rowland, timidly, uncertain if his host wished to be included in the conversation.

"I suffered a deuced shattering detour round Rheims and Fontainbeleau—to discourage an undesirable following, you understand," responded the Duke, bestowing a significant glance upon Isabella whose colour heightened considerably.

"Did any young beau have the presumption to propose, your ladyship?" Rowland pursued, discretion overcome with curiosity as his eyes shuttled back and forth between brother and sister.

Isabella glanced instinctively at her brother, expecting him to assume command, before replying hurriedly: "N-Not really—but I was in such great demand wherever I went—"

"Naturally, with your fortune," broke in the Duke, oblivious to her poisonous look as he strove to stifle a yawn.

But Isabella continued undeterred. "I swear, gentlemen,

I enjoyed myself so much, Gideon had to quite drag me back home!"

This struck Rowland as downright ludicrous and his efforts to suppress a laugh resulted in a rather peculiar cough.

The Viscount could contain his anxiety no longer. "M-My lady, did you favour any suitor?"

"No!" interposed her brother, emphatically.

"I am perfectly able to answer for myself, Gideon!" she rejoined tartly. "And I might add, matrimony may be distasteful to you but it is not so to me! It will serve you right if I'm left on your hands, a rejected relic!"

"They were fortune hunters, m' dear," he drawled, nonchalantly regarding the priceless rings on his fingers. "You will thank me one day for interceding." He glanced significantly at the Viscount, which had a miraculous quelling effect upon her ladyship, before he turned back to the window, to gaze through heavy-lidded eyes at the passing moonlit countryside—the very effort seeming to overtire him.

Rowland here, with a surreptitious glance at the Duke, leaned across to enquire of the Viscount, in a discreet whisper: "Has Gideon never wished to marry and settle down?"

The Viscount likewise flashed a look at his friend—who now gave every impression of being asleep—before ceding to Rowland's curiosity in the same hushed tone.

"He almost did, a number of years ago, but I'm not sure—"

"G-Gideon?" gasped her ladyship, sitting up with a start, her Parisian season forgotten. "Al—almost wed?"

"Sh-sh," urged Lord Sevington, who would have preferred to leave the matter there, but the feverish interest established on the faces of his audience—and the assurance that the Duke was indeed sleeping—compelled him to go on, with Isabella agog in front, and Rowland equally agog on his right.

"It happened just before Gideon gained his majority and immense fortune," he resumed in low tone, their heads bowed together as if plotting high-treason, "that he met an exceptionally beautiful young woman named Eugenia, with whom he fell instantly in love. Granted, she was some four years his senior, but he was always mature beyond his age. Howbeit, she in turn fully reciprocated his love, and during this time there was no happier man on earth."

He paused for breath, colouring slightly at Isabella's unashamed gaze as she hung on his every word—as he had hung upon hers.

"Where she came from she would not say—her origin being rather dubious—but vowed she had no surviving relative. Because of this, she prevailed upon Gideon to keep their love secret as his mother, the Dowager Duchess, would do all in her power to put an end to their association. The result was an elopement, known only to the couple and myself."

Again his eyes flickered nervously in the Duke's vicinity, but his Grace was oblivious to all, with his hat obscuring both eyes.

"Yes? Yes?" prompted Rowland, impatiently.

"They had not been gone more than two hours when a gentleman of breeding arrived to enquire where his Grace could be found as he had vital business with him. I explained that the Duke was away from home—at which he became extremely agitated and begged to confide in me, on the assurance that I was his closest friend. It was then that he introduced himself. He was none other than Sir Roger Tremayne—Eugenia's husband."

His listeners gasped aloud in dismay.

"Needless to say, Sir Roger and I set out post haste after them—and as Gideon had fortunately confided to me where the clandestine ceremony was to take place, we were able to arrive on time. The moment Eugenia set eyes on her husband she knew that all was lost, and fled. She has not been seen again—as far as I know."

Having ended his narrative, Lord Sevington passed a well-manicured hand across his forehead in recollection of the nightmare, as a breathless hush fell—broken suddenly by a muffled but unmistakable snore from beneath the Duke's hat.

"What a heart-rending story," faltered Rowland tragically, recovering his voice at this point.

But he was by no means the more stricken of the two.

"Oh—oh, my lord," whispered Isabella brokenly, laying a trembling hand upon the Viscount's satin-clad arm. "Why has Gideon never told me all this?"

His lordship covered her hand with his, accelerating his heartbeat.

"It was too painful an episode in his life, Lady Isabella, which he does not care to recall," he smiled, sympathetically.

Smiling modestly up at him, Isabella forced back her tears and sat back, but with her high spirits greatly subdued.

And so they jogged along, on their seemingly endless journey to the Duke's country seat in Wiltshire, silent awhile, each having much to occupy their thoughts—until the Duke roused with a yawn, when the Viscount tactfully introduced a new topic of conversation.

"Is there much unrest in France, Gideon?" he queried, sociably.

"No more than usual," returned the other, lackadaisically. "But as I did not expend a deal of time carousing with the local peasantry, I'm afraid my opinion is not to be relied upon."

In this strain the conversation progressed, comparing safe old England with restless France. But was England so safe?

Politically, perhaps—but out in the eerie stillness, where the moon bedappled the countryside with sinister black shadows, and the dark forest loomed ahead—famed as a refuge for gentlemen of the High Toby—thieves and rogues who would not cavil at slitting a throat or two, or blowing out a few brains for nothing more than a handful of guineas or a buckle off a shoe—waiting . . . pistols primed and at the ready to ambush an unwary traveller.

But the little group of aristocrats continued merrily on their way in blissful ignorance, refusing to acknowledge the possibility of a hold-up so near to their destination. So confident were they, that Mr. Chalmers was asking her ladyship if she really was not thankful, after all, to be back in her peaceful little England—when a pistol shot rang out, to split the night asunder and set to flight a host of terror-stricken birds.

A second shot resounded before a coarse impatient voice demanded: "Stand an' deliver!"

The petrified coachman complied as speedily as possible, and the coach gave a lurch as it ground to a halt with no little discomfort to its distinguished passengers.

"What the devil's going on?" exclaimed Rowland indignantly, thrusting his bewigged head out of the window only to hastily withdraw it again as the muzzle of a long-barrelled pistol met his vision, at the extreme end of which stood a tall, black, disagreeable-looking figure.

"Come on! Don't sit there gawpin'!" it barked roughly. " 'And over the gew-gaws! 'Urry it up, there!"

Three of his victims, deeming it safer to submit, reluctantly began gathering together their valuables and relinquishing them into his covetous hands, while his accomplice (who not only lacked his audacity but seemed rather nervous) tried to hide behind his colleague and, at the same time, keep the coachman in check at the point of his not-too-steady pistol. Suddenly, a third shot reverberated in the night, and reeling in the saddle, the highwayman fell heavily to the ground, scattering jewels on the way, to lie writhing in agony, clutching frantically at his left shoulder, whilst the Duke still lounged, his aristocratic hand toying with—not an eye-glass—but a small silver-chased pistol.

A piercing scream erupted from the accomplice, and hurling himself from his frightened horse, he collapsed beside his friend, crying in a broken young voice: "Bart! Oh, Bart!"

"G-Get ye gone!" gasped the sufferer. "Go . . . wh-whilst ye . . . can."

"No, Bart! No! Never! Never!" protested the other, stubbornly.

Isabella, having sat transfixed throughout the tragedy, here uttered in dismay: "Gideon—he's only a boy!"—and wrenching open the coach door, leapt out before anyone could stop her, harbouring no concern for her exquisite Parisian gown and cloak of scarlet velvet and ermine trailing in the dust, as she knelt beside the young man, a comforting hand on his heaving shoulder.

"I-Is he badly hurt?" she breathed anxiously. "I'm sure

my brother didn't mean to harm him—just frighten him off."

Meanwhile, Lord Sevington, who had followed swiftly in her wake, now discovered he could do little but hover over her, reiterating: "Come, my lady—there is nothing you can do."

But they were both due for a further shock as the young man snatched away hat and mask to reveal a young and extremely beautiful girl. Golden hair rippled down to her waist, framing a face unbelievable in its perfection. The skin—creamy and satin-smooth, the nose—short and straight, the lips—red, delectable and well-shaped, while the eyes, large and soulful and of a profound blue, alas for their owner, usually evoked jealousy in women and lechery in men. But in Isabella they evoked only the deepest compassion, as they gazed up at her in desperation.

"Oh, please help me, m' lady?" she pleaded wildly, baring the wound and making an admirable attempt to staunch the blood.

"Y-Yes—yes indeed! I'll help you," vowed Isabella—to the Viscount's further disconcertion.

"B-But Lady Isabella!" he expostulated. "Y-You can't! What will Gideon say?"

"That is what I am now going to find out," she replied forcefully, rising to her feet to stalk boldly back to the coach.

Her brother was inhaling a pinch of snuff with due ceremony when she appeared at the coach door, with Lord Sevington's protests vibrating in her ears.

The Duke cast her an enquiring glance, snuff-box elegantly poised. "Here for the night, 'Bella?"

"What do you intend doing for this poor man you have

almost killed?" she demanded, as if this ruthless scoundrel who had threatened them all with similar treatment not two minutes ago were now exonerated of all blame by a ball in the shoulder.

"What would you suggest?" he parried, dryly.

"I suggest you get him to a surgeon—at once!"

The overwhelming effect this statement was supposed to have completely misfired. Instead, he closed his snuff-box with a snap and sat awhile rapt in admiration of its enamel-and-gold motif, before dusting particles of snuff from his magnificent full-skirted, huge-cuffed coat of emerald velvet with languid waves of his hand. Only when fully satisfied with his appearance did he turn his contemptuous gaze upon her, pocketing the snuff-box.

"And which surgeon have you in mind?"

The unexpected question threw her into confusion. "I-I'm afraid I don't know of any in particular," she confessed, ruefully.

"Precisely, 'Bella. The only one that happens to reside in the area is my own physician, who won't reach Wiltshire for another two days. What do you suggest I do now?" he continued with biting disdain, "—take him home and tend his wound myself?"

"P-Please, Gideon!" she begged pitifully, resorting to a change of technique. "W-Won't you do something?"

"How dramatic!" he mocked. "My dear sister pleading for the worthless life of a common felon. Ha' done with the theatricals—they give me the melancholy!"

"But if—"

" 'Bella! If I were to take compassion on all my unfortunate victims I'd be governing a confounded hospital."

"But if only for the girl's sake. . . ."

"Girl?" he enquired in idle interest. "What girl?"

"His companion—he isn't a boy at all! He—er—she's a girl!"

He eyed her in cynical amusement. "Is the shortage of males so acute in the vicinity that they are obliged to accept females into the profession? Faith—had I but known," he added, facetiously, "I might have volunteered."

A nervous laugh escaped Rowland despite the grave situation, but her ladyship was far from humoured by her brother's empty jest.

"Very well, 'Bella," he sighed finally, bored by the whole episode. "Bring the wench here."

Rowland, having sat mumchance throughout this exchange, here offered a suggestion.

"We can't be far from your—er—place, now, Gideon," he submitted dubiously. "Perhaps I could take one of the team, ride on ahead, and bring back a chaise or something to take the fellow to a doctor—but 'fraid I don't know where the next one lives . . . probably wouldn't need one time I got him there."

"I don't think that will be necessary, Rowland," returned his Grace, suppressing a smile—hesitating as his gaze fell upon the vision at the door, her tears now subsided.

Very slowly did the Duke lower his feet to the floor and sit up, interest awakened, motioning her to enter and be seated, which she did—cautiously, twisting her battered tricorne agitatedly in her hands (when not whisking stray tears from her cheeks). The girl flushed deeply as his cold green eyes stripped her from top to toe, remarking the multi-patched coat with torn pocket, the tattered remnants crying out to be a waistcoat, knee-breeches minus knees, crudely-shod stockingless feet, and threadbare shirt, beneath which he perceived the voluptuous fullness of a well-matured female form. Even had she not been pre-occupied with her recent trouble, she would never have discerned her effect upon him. Only by the firmness of his mouth and the way his long fingers gripped the armrest, could it possibly be detected—which she was too dis-traught to notice. It was not the incomparable beauty of her which played havoc with the Duke's self-control, but something more profound—capable of rousing his long-dormant passion.

His lips curled into the sardonic sneer he invariably held at the ready, and a malicious look of self-satisfaction overspread his countenance.

"Well . . ." he purred, like a cat having run a fat juicy mouse to earth. " 'Twould seem Dame Fortune has at last smiled my way."

"Oh, p-please, sir—I-I implore you," she burst out in anguish. "Don't leave my brother out here to d-die!"

"Where would you prefer him to die?" he flung back, scornfully. "In my lap?"

With a gasp of horror she shrank back into the red plush seat, painfully aware that if her brother's life was not to be sacrificed she must do her utmost to humour this cruel individual.

"And your name, I presume, is Melpomene," he re-sumed with satire, indifferent to her feelings, "—after the Goddess of Tragedy?"

"My name, sir, is Rosalind," she replied in surprisingly steady voice, suppressing her disgust as she strove to guard her tongue—though unable to stop herself adding: "—after no one!"

His eyes narrowed dangerously. "Ah! Methinks I detect the defiance of an untamed filly." He lounged back, idly twirling his eye-glass round by its ribbon. "I am plagued with ennui, and cherish a fancy for entertainment. No doubt you possess powers of persuasion equal to the rest of your sex? Very well—persuade me! If you give a commendable performance, I may be tempted to take a lenient view of your misdemeanour."

Rosalind stared at him, bewildered. "P-Persuade you, sir? H-How?"

The sardonic sneer became more pronounced. "To be blunt, tell me precisely what I have to gain by sparing your miserable carcasses."

It did not take long to dawn upon her what any man would be interested in gaining from a young female like herself, and so swallowing pride and scruples, she faltered: "I-I will sac-sacrifice anything . . . to s-save my . . . b-brother."

"Anything?" he stressed, ominously.

Rosalind hung her head, devoured with shame at thoughts of the terrible fate she was outlining for herself.

"You perchance think me in such desperate need for female companionship as to avail myself of your so generous offer?"

Not knowing what else she could offer, she merely stared forlornly down at the hat in her hands—now twisted out of all recognition, whilst Rowland Chalmers —whose lace ruffles at his throat appeared to have shrunk two inches—gave a discreet cough, not daring to interfere. Even Isabella opened her mouth to protest, closed it again, realising the danger in provoking her brother in his present mood.

"And if I did," went on the Duke, "what guarantee have you that I should keep my part of the bargain?"

"N-None," she was forced to acknowledge.

"Quite!" he concurred, a fiendish glint in his eye as his voice dropped to a menacing snarl. "Nevertheless—despair not, my hapless brigand! You fulfil my requirements to perfection—and you will be sacrificed—make no mistake on that score—but not how you imagine!" He savoured his moment of triumph awhile before addressing his sister. "Have the wretch brought in, 'Bella!"

In a mixture of surprise and suspicion, her ladyship hastened away to execute his order ere he could change his mind, and outside her excited voice was soon raised in authority, whereby Bart was borne into the coach and laid to rest with his head cradled in his sister's lap—everyone thankful that he had lost consciousness.

2

The rest of the journey was completed beneath a pall of silence. Lord Sevington knitted his fair brows—certain he had seen the girl before, but being unable to boast even the remotest association with the criminal world, could not admit to the possibility. Rowland also rattled his brains—wondering why the Duke was going to all this trouble on behalf of two common felons—particularly the villainous Bart! Surely he did not mean to preserve the scoundrel's life after trying to do away with it? After all, it could have been any one of them—even Gideon himself—lying there wounded had they chanced to resist the fellow's demands. But even Rowland's strict law-abiding conscience suffered a pang as his eyes rested on Rosalind. She was only a child when all was said and done, and had more than likely been coerced into the dastardly game by that cut-throat brother of hers—and he had to confess, she was damned attractive! Ah!—was that Gideon's motive? He readily admitted his inability to interpret the Duke's cryptic remarks, but in this case the terms 'persuasion' and 'sacrifice' could mean only one thing—that his intentions were far from honourable. He tut-tutted to himself in disapproval, but ultimately vindicated his conscience by vowing the fate a better one than dancing on the end of a rope at Tyburn, which the girl herself would be first to agree.

Howbeit, Rosalind was labouring under the worst strain of all—beginning to wonder if she had not acted a little too precipitately by craving the assistance of these strangers and so placed herself and Bart in a more pre-carious position than ever. As her over-bearing captor had already stated, what guarantee had she that he would help her even if she did as he wished? Unfortunately, she was unable to glean much information about her com-panions, as they used only first names and made no mention of their destination.

Eventually, they passed through the great gates of the Duke's country seat, and up the five-mile drive through extensive grounds ere the huge Palladian residence loomed into view—though little could be distinguished in the moonlight. The coach glided to a halt at the foot of the steps, overshadowed by a thirty-foot-high pillared portico, where the Duke alighted to be warmly welcomed by Rowland's plain but personable wife, Fiona, and a multi-tude of servants. Inside the grand entrance hall, which was ablaze with chandeliers, white Italian marble and gold, servants were scurrying to and fro, two bearing the wounded Bart away in company with his awe-inspired sister, to a distant part of the house, followed by Paul—the Duke's valet—who had (on occasion) acted as sur-geon for his master, and now looked about to do so again.

The company—adjourning to their rooms to refresh themselves for a belated dinner—gave Fiona Chalmers her desired chance to pounce on her husband (admiring him-self in the nearest mirror) with a volley of questions about the two 'revolting creatures'—alas, only to find her spouse infuriatingly in the dark, knowing little more than the obvious. This prompted her long thin face to fall even longer as she tugged irritably at her newly-frizzed auburn hair, her curiosity fully alerted—and determined to have it satisfied at the earliest opportunity.

Not surprisingly, the hold-up was the main topic of conversation during the meal, and Fiona—having acquired the gist of it from her husband—was now deeply engrossed in Isabella's version, intensified with morbid detail, while the gentlemen made apposite comments upon the increasing number of highway robberies of late.

"That cook of yours can certainly do justice to a partridge, Gideon," declared Rowland, injecting a lighter vein into the discourse. "I'v never tasted better!"

His host smiled his acknowledgment.

"I vow throughout the last few miles of the ghastly journey my hunger became most acute," continued the other, his hand involuntarily patting the relevant part of his anatomy, whilst the rest of the company echoed his statement.

Peace reigned over the table awhile, the footmen treading soundlessly about, replenishing wine-glasses and empty platters, the gold plate glinting in the candlelight—until her ladyship shattered the silence.

"Fancy being a highwaywoman!" she breathed, on an unmistakable note of envy. "What a marvelous idea! I wish I'd thought of it!"

Lord Sevington choked rather violently, while her brother merely threw her a look of disgust.

"Er—I s'pose by now you'll have sent a servant hot-foot to notify the authorities, Gideon?" opined Rowland in a matter-of-fact tone, while the Viscount strove to recover himself—this casual observation having a disconcerting effect on Isabella.

"Loth as I am to disappoint you, Rowland—alas, I have not," returned his Grace, urbanely.

"No? . . . Oh, well! P'raps there's time yet—but harbouring criminals, y'know—dangerous offence! If news got abroad—hmm—servants—can't keep their confounded tongues still!" he explained, a little uncertain how this would be received.

"Do you really mean to hand them over to the law, Gideon?" probed Isabella, trying to quell the urgency in her voice.

The Duke hesitated, viewing with a critical eye a dish of sweetmeats in front of him. "I'm afraid I haven't yet given the matter much thought."

"Surely it requires no thought?" cut in the Viscount, astonished. "Your legal course of action is perfectly clear."

"Legal? You perchance see me as a devout upholder of law and order, m' dear fellow?" he mused, pleased with the analogy.

"But think of the scandal attached to shielding these offenders!"

The Duke heaved a sigh. "Does my wealth and position bear such little consequence these days?"

"Hum—forgive me," mumbled his lordship, "but it was your repute—"

"Ah—yes, Chris!" accorded his friend, amiably. "My unenviable reputation—I had almost forgotten. Mayhap you would care to wager the outcome—my reputation against . . . hmm . . . against your chances of marrying 'Bella!"—and he rounded off his proposition by bestowing a brotherly smile on Isabella and another sugarplum into his mouth.

"Gideon!" she vituperated, reddening to the hue of the Viscount's claret coat—whilst the latter's attempt to hide his discomfort was a trifle more successful. "I think you are perfectly horrid!"

"I'm inclined to agree, m' dear," he concurred, unperturbed. "You must excuse my bizarre sense of humour."

He paused to dabble his beringed fingers in a silver finger-bowl, before wiping them with meticulous care—whilst his sister smouldered like a volcano.

"And if you don't give them up to the law," she snapped, sullenly, "what will you do with them?"

"Brother Bart in no wise merits my interest," he replied dryly, discarding his banter. "He should have abandoned this life an hour since were it not for his sister."

"And his sister?" she pressed him, voicing the question for everyone.

The Duke provoked their suspense to screaming pitch by first taking a lingering sip of wine.

"His sister? Well . . . she might relieve my boredom occasionally."

"I should prefer to hang if I were she!" was Isabella's stinging rejoinder.

"Perchance she values her existence the greater," he parried, calmly.

Her ladyship smarted 'neath the gibe, wishing she could resist the impulse to pit her wits against her brother's. Whilst she fought to regain her composure, Fiona besought her host.

"Y-Your Grace—I beg you to think before doing anything rash. This girl—this child—is no older than your own sister." She smiled significantly at Isabella (who struggled to assume a supplicating expression solely for her brother's benefit) before flashing her spouse a warning look, defying him to gainsay her.

As everyone had voiced their opinion on the matter, they all now looked to Rowland to voice his—who felt obliged to support his wife, and so shelving his principles concerning the law, petitioned the Duke, unpretentiously.

"I pray you will consider, Gideon, not simply the bare facts, but the ethics of a gentleman. I feel no one must be more acutely aware of the unforgivable crime which has been committed than the girl herself, and while I fully appreciate your merciful attitude in refraining to notify the law, a gentleman must bear in mind that, though she may not aspire to our level, she is, nevertheless, a member of the fair sex and, particularly as a child, should be honoured as such."

This feat of eloquence filled Fiona with pride and she accordingly beamed her approval on her gallant spouse, whilst excitement welled up in Isabella, that her brother—now well and truly cornered—must openly state his intentions or insult the company. But once again she underestimated him.

"Your oratorical powers are a never-ending source of delight, Rowland," he drawled, unenthusiastically. "However, I was under the impression that you strongly advocated sending a servant hot-foot to notify the authorities?"

Rowland emitted a strangled cry as the pointed toe of his wife's shoe penetrated his left shin, in repayment for his stupidity—her pride evidently short-lived.

"W-Well . . . I-I—er—" began Rowland, decidedly uncomfortable, sandwiched between his irate wife and his perspicacious host.

"Apart from which," resumed the Duke with amicable candour, "I cannot for the life of me comprehend why anyone of intelligence and elevated status should concern themselves to such an absurd degree on behalf of two such misbegotten blackguards."

This put paid to any further discourse upon the subject, no one wishing to be thought lacking in intelligence, and so the ladies—abandoning all hope of squeezing the Duke of any further information—betook themselves to the small drawing-room, leaving the gentlemen to their wine —where they were at liberty to chatter without fear of interruption, or contradiction.

Whilst the gathering dined below, Paul and Rosalind waged a strenuous battle for the life of Bart, who fortunately remained unconscious throughout the arduous operation. But their exertions were eventually rewarded and Bart lay clothed in a white nightshirt, at peace with the world, looking as angelic as he probably ever would. Rosalind tried to express her gratitude, but the valet respectfully waived it aside, and picking up his bundle of peculiar instruments, drew her attention to a bottle of sack by the bed, before leaving to report the outcome of his efforts to his Grace.

No sooner had the door closed than Rosalind fell weakly on to the tripod stool by the dresser, having sustained yet another shock—that her keeper was a duke—and there being only one in the area meant he must be the infamous Delvray! The style of address had fallen so naturally from the valet's lips that he had been quite unaware of it.

Her first question was to ask herself in what way it was to his advantage to succour a pair of criminals? There was a motive of some kind, for had not he stated most emphatically that she would indeed be sacrificed?—but not in the way she expected . . . so she could not be destined for his bed or the gallows. How, then, was she to be sacrificed?

Cupping her chin in her hand, she gazed critically at her reflection in the ivory-framed mirror. What she saw apparently did not please her, for the frown deepened considerably, marring still further the features already testifying to the rigorous ordeal she had undergone. Flashing a glance at the inert Bart, she tried to determine what he would say when he eventually awoke, in full appreciation of their situation. He would probably begin by reproaching himself for getting her into this mess, but Rosalind knew deep down that she had no one but herself to blame. Bart had warned her scores of times what would happen if they were ever caught—even she would be shown no mercy at the hands of the law. It had taken all her cajoling and wheedling to persuade him to take her with him, and, even then, had tried to dissuade her ever since. But she was young and adventuresome, and was borne away with the thrills and excitement until she was helpless to resist. And so, she ruminated their precarious position, unaware that her head was growing heavier and heavier, until it dropped on to her folded arms, and with a final murmur she fell asleep.

3

Following dinner, Rowland and Fiona retired for the night, leaving her ladyship still agog with curiosity, the Viscount submerged in thought, and the Duke sprawled in a chair by the fire, extremely satisfied with life and what it held in store.

Silence prevailed, which Isabella put to good use by casting coquettish glances at his lordship, distracting him sufficiently to smile back at her—none of which passed unnoticed by the Duke.

"I doubt if your ogling will bear much fruit tonight, 'Bella," he drawled, with a knowing look. "Chris would appear to have more vital issues weighing on his mind, to play the amorous swain."

Her ladyship flushed indignantly. "So indeed have we all, brother dear, which only you can enlighten, when it please you."

"Faith! If you dally solely on the offchance of having your feline curiosity satisfied—alas, I must disappoint you. On the contrary, a good night's rest would benefit you prodigiously. After that hectic trip you look thoroughly washed-up."

What could her ladyship do but exit with a good grace? And so, with a rueful good night to Lord Sevington—who leapt afoot to bow over her dainty hand—she reluctantly quitted the room.

The Viscount returned to his chair and for some time only the crackling of burning logs and the ticking of the gilt ornamental clock on the mantelshelf above, were all that disturbed the serenity of the room—his lordship fidgeting with his wine-glass, as he gazed abstractedly into the fire, while his companion reached out a hand, partially concealed by a cascade of finest Mechlin lace, to select himself a comfit from a nearby dish.

"Would you care to relieve your emotions on one of my less valuable pieces, Chris?"

The Viscount sat up with a start to stare down at the treasure resting in his hands, as if wondering how it came to be there, and at once placed it carefully by the sweetmeat bowl, with a nervous smile.

"F-Forgive me, Gideon," he faltered. "I seem to be a trifle unnerved."

The Duke reclined at ease, in idle contemplation of an amply proportioned nymph portrayed upon the high ceiling, as he observed: "Which, o' course, has no connection whatever with my fair felon."

Lord Sevington cleared his throat sheepishly, to admit: "I-It's just that I can't think why you're bothering to preserve the life of that Bart! I mean, if all you wanted was the girl, why didn't you just take her?"

" 'Pon rep! And risk a scene like all Bedlam let loose?" ejaculated his Grace aghast. "Really, my dear fellow, you have no idea how some females take on at such times— or have you?"

The Viscount ignored the quip.

"It was quite obvious the girl and he were wholly inseparable, so in order to avoid any unpleasantness— er—screaming and the like—not to mention actual physical violence which has resulted on occasion—I deigned to nurse the ruffian back to health."

"You—hum—must want her passing-well to go to such lengths."

The Duke eyed his friend strangely, his eyes glowing greener than usual. "I do indeed, my dear Chris," he acknowledged in sinister tone—almost evil. "One might even say—with a vengeance!"

"O-Oddly enough," stammered the Viscount, experiencing some discomfort, "I have a feeling I've seen her before, some . . . where—"

He broke off as a laugh escaped the Duke—a laugh of Satan—which caused his lordship to shift uneasily in his chair. Neither did he care for the infernal look overspreading his friend's eminent countenance—it boded ill. But the Duke unexpectedly cast his mood from him like a cloak, and rising unhurriedly to his feet, drew himself up to his full six feet three inches to stroll, with a rustle of his ice-blue satin coat, trimmed with silver-lace, across to the beechwood wine-cabinet on the far wall, where he selected a wine to his liking—his black hair (the sole item of his dress to defy the fashionable trend) draping his shoulders and stressing to advantage the pallor of his inscrutable face.

"You surprise me, Chris!" he exclaimed with a touch of satire. "Your memory is usually quite retentive—but in this instance, mine is even better. Shall I issue an official proclamation—or will a few discreet innuendoes suffice?" His jocular tone changed suddenly to searing contempt. "Having entertained us all en route with your dramatic recital of my intimate past, I'm even more surprised you aren't already six jumps ahead of me!"

The Viscount stared at him blankly, obviously still in the dark.

"Damn it all, Chris! Must I spell it out for you? Doesn't

she remind you of anyone—someone of whom I for one do not care to be reminded?"

If his lordship had been slapped across his charming face, he could not have looked more stupefied. "Eu—Eugenia!" he gasped. "Gideon, h-how on earth could I have been so blind?"

The Duke returned to his chair, making no further comment.

"But how could I fail to . . ." The Viscount's voice trailed away as he sank his head between his hands, striving to rally his bewildered thoughts, while his host lay slumped in his chair, his face a death-mask but for his eyes which smouldered venomously.

Eventually, Lord Sevington raised his head to fix his gaze on the Duke's face. "I see now that the resemblance is unmistakable."

"There seems little doubt to me that she's Eugenia's offspring!"

The Viscount nodded. "You—er—think you can prove it?"

"I intend to try," responded his Grace, laconically.

"How old do you think she is—about—hum—seventeen?"

The Duke shrugged. "Maybe a little older—which makes it abundantly clear," he went on, forestalling his friend, "that she was very much alive at the time of the nuptial farce!"

"Er—exactly—and—hum—might feasibly be of gentle birth should she turn out to be the legitimate daughter of Sir Roger."

A sneer curled the Duke's lips. "That sows an irrepressible seed of doubt in my mind, having known her mother so well."

They lapsed awhile into silence, the contrast between the two long-standing friends more marked than usual—their only common factor being a similarity of height.

"I should be obliged, Chris, if, for the moment, this matter could be kept strictly to ourselves," requested the Duke, gently.

"Of course, Gideon—no need to ask!" declared the other, fervently, furthering the avowal with a husky remark about appreciating the delicate situation. Another minute ticked by before he found courage to add—clearing his throat, with a wary glance: "The—hum—girl—d-do you really m-mean to . . . er . . ."

"Seduce her?" supplied his Grace, amicably—his friend wincing. "Hm-m—not tonight, m' dear fellow. I simply haven't the energy!"—and suiting action to words, yawned, struggling to his feet, to propose 'bed' to a somewhat sceptical Viscount.

Meanwhile, a tap upon the door, though gentle, made Rosalind start from her slumbers and jump afoot in alarm, her heart pounding in her breast as the door slowly opened —she fully expecting to see the tall impressive figure of the Duke standing on the threshold, having come to claim compensation for his so generous assistance. But the face with the shy, apprehensive smile, which peered round, evoked an audible sigh of relief from her, ere she bade her visitor welcome.

Isabella tripped lightly in, closing the door behind her, discreetly choosing to ignore Rosalind's expression—but mentally drawing her own conclusions. Having collided with a footman bearing a tray thither, she seized upon the idea to take the tray herself as an excuse to gain admittance and answers to some pertinent questions.

"I felt certain you would be hungry," she said simply,

placing the tray upon the table, by the wine-bottle.

"Th-thank you, m-my lady, but—"

Isabella gestured her stammered gratitude aside. "You may show your appreciation by telling me how your brother does."

Rosalind eagerly obliged, stating all that was necessary, then fell silent, overcome with embarrassment at the elegance of her ladyship in her priceless gown of apple-green silk and cream lace, fashioned *à la mode* from Paris. And glancing down at her own masculine rags, suddenly recalled her manners, and again proffered her thanks whilst endeavouring to drop a curtsy. Nervously twisting her fingers, she then burst out, agitatedly: "M-My lady—I can think of no reason why his Grace should help my brother and I, a-after the terrible thing we've done. . . . I should be even d-deeper in your debt if you would off-offer him . . . m-my . . . thanks."

Isabella smiled dubiously. "Your gratitude may yet be rather premature, Rosalind, as no one—not even I myself —can say what my brother intends." Striving to curb the curiosity in her voice, she added: "I gather the Duke has given no intimation at all regarding your immediate future?"

"None, your ladyship—b-but should he d-decide to t-turn us over . . . to the l-law, it is no m-more than w-we deserve, and . . . sp-speaking for m-myself . . . I-I would try as b-bravely . . . as p-possible to f-face . . . m-my just . . . p-pun . . . ish . . . ment."

This gallant little speech slowly trailed away, ending in a pitiful inarticulation, prompting Isabella to leap once again to the defence of this poor creature.

"I forbid you to entertain such a dreadful thought!" she cried aghast, placing an arm round Rosalind's trembling shoulders. "I'm sure even Gideon—as heartless as he sometimes is—wouldn't stoop so low as to betray a young defenceless girl like yourself."

These words had the comforting effect desired, and presently her ladyship was rewarded with a tremulous smile.

"I suggest you have your supper and go to bed," she went on, in maternal fashion. "Is there anything else you need?" Receiving a negative reply, she proceeded to the door. "Then I shall bid you good night—and pray do not alarm yourself."

With a sympathetic smile she was gone, leaving Rosalind to avail herself of her sound advice.

4

Although Rosalind found her every need attended to at the Duke's palatial home, no reference was made throughout the following week to her future, or Bart's, who—to her delight—was making steady progress, having accepted the irregular situation and his sumptuous surroundings with a tolerance and understanding she had thought utterly beyond his mental capabilities, considering them both extremely lucky to have their necks still intact.

In fact, it was not until Bart was almost recovered some two weeks later, and Rowland and Fiona had departed for home (the latter, only on condition that her ladyship kept her informed of any developments at Claremont Park) that the Duke deemed the moment opportune to summon Rosalind to his presence—whilst his sister demonstrated her skill upon the hapischord in the music salon, for the benefit of Lord Sevington—his lordship, perhaps, more entranced with her charming self than her merely tolerable performance.

The Duke awaited Rosalind in the library, submerged in a Tudor chair, idly swinging one white silk-bestockinged leg over the other, his tall manly figure adorned in a coat of the finest crimson brocade, 'neath which he sported a gold-embroidered waistcoat. Lethargically, he helped himself to his favourite snuff, closing the bejewelled box as a timid knock sounded upon the door.

"Enter," he drawled, returning the box to his pocket. The door opened by degrees, and when wide enough to admit a human form, Rosalind sidled in, closing it behind her to stand with her back to it, devoured with apprehension, gazing about the room in some confusion as it appeared to be completely deserted—until the unmistakable voice of the Duke issued from the chair on her immediate right.

"Come here."

Gingerly, she approached, keeping a distance—which did not escape his notice.

"I indulge in numerable vices," he sardonically apprised her, "but rest content, biting isn't one of them."

He indicated a chair, upon which she cautiously perched, her eyes roaming about the room in awe at the priceless array of volumes covering the walls from floor to ceiling—punctuated by notable works of art by artists of the day, the like of which she had never seen before. The Duke regarded her shrewdly the while in silence, allowing her to gaze her fill of the splendours of his house, after which he anticipated she might devote her mind all the better to the vital issue at stake.

Eventually, her eyes fell to his face where they did not linger very long before dropping self-consciously to her feet.

"Now we can talk," he proposed with languid amicability. "Or rather, *you* can talk. I shall do nothing more strenuous than listen."

"Wh-what shall I talk about, your Grace?" she faltered.

The Duke heaved a sigh. "Well, child, I did not have you summoned hither to hold discourse upon the weather. I wish to hear your life history from as far back as you remember."

She flashed a questioning look at him, but it availed her nought. "There isn't much to tell, your Grace."

He gave no sign of having heard her, or made any effort to put her at ease and seemingly did not intend to —so, fixing her eyes upon a Hogarth painting on the opposite wall, she began.

"I was imprisoned in a convent—"

"Imprisoned?" he prompted in mild surprise.

"Well, your Grace, I saw little difference when I was—"

"As you will," he acknowledged with a brief gesture, appreciating a lengthy explanation was involved. "Pray continue."

"I was there until four years ago when I—er—r-ran away"—she flashed a glance to see how this had shocked him, but he didn't seem shocked at all. "Somehow I lost my way when it grew dark and so sought shelter at a cottage—intending to stay only the night, but the people were very kind and begged me to stay—"

"Being brother Bart and his family, I presume?"

"Y-Yes."

An awkward silence ensued, the Duke patiently waiting for her to resume.

"Well?" he ventured at length, throwing her a look of enquiry. "Is that all?"

"Yes, your Grace."

He eyed her with scepticism, but let it pass, and fired a question at random. "What do you know of your parents?"

She gave a hopeless sigh. "Nothing, I'm afraid—I don't even know my full name. I've always thought myself an orphan like the rest of the children at the convent. My parents were never mentioned." On afterthought, she began to remove a finely-wrought gold chain from about her neck, which she proffered to him. "I have this, if it's of any help. I was told it belonged to my mother."

The Duke took the chain calmly, and examined it with

feigned unconcern, belying the passion of hatred which welled up in him, as upon the chain hung a locket inscribed with his own initials entwined with Eugenia's— one of his premarital gifts to her. If he harboured any doubts about Rosalind, they were now entirely dispelled. He returned it with a perfectly steady hand, making no comment, then viewed her with renewed interest—a look she nobly fought to meet, in an effort to determine what was coming next.

"This convent," he queried, curiously. "Where is it?"

Her brows drew together in concentration. "About forty miles due west. It's called the Convent of the Blessed Martyrs."

"How very apt," he murmured to himself. "Where they gave you a tolerable education."

"Oh, yes! I can boast a number of accomplishments, your Grace."

He was not impressed. "Don't you deem it somewhat irregular—irrespective of the danger—for a young female of your standards to be frolicking about the countryside in such a manner?"

All at once she felt ashamed, and coloured profusely, nervously clearing her throat. "We-ll—it was Bart's idea originally . . . y-you see, we had to think of something . . . his people were very poor—and we tried to find work in the neighbourhood, but nobody seemed to w-want . . . B-Bart."

Her implication immediately roused his interest. "And yourself?"

Rosalind gnawed her bottom lip, devoured with humiliation. "I d-did not . . . favour their . . . p-prop . . . osals. . . ."

"Which would have solved your difficulties, nonetheless," he pointed out, suavely, "—with your endowment of—er—charms. . . ."

If she nurtured any misunderstanding about his interpretation, his eyes made it abundantly plain.

"I'd rather hang!" she burst out, her eyes flashing—echoing her ladyship's opinion on the matter.

"An admirable sentiment, I grant you—but not a very wise one."

Amused lazy green eyes held smouldering blue for one tense moment, a significant smile playing round his lips.

"I take it, the High Toby was your only alternative?" he appended, cynically.

"Yes," she replied, innocently. "Apart from deliberately stealing."

This statement elevated one of his delicately pencilled brows. "There's a difference, of course?" he returned in some surprise.

But Rosalind seemed just as surprised that he should doubt it.

"Most certainly, your Grace!" she cried with indignation—evidently a subject she felt strongly about. Strong enough, in fact, to cast her prior diffidence to the winds. "Indeed, you do us grave injustice to think that we would openly steal from anyone who could ill afford it! It was our code to rob only the rich like yourself, who—if you'll pardon me—"

"Granted."

"—would miss a purseful of jewels as sorely as a handful of leaves from the trees on their estates!"

"Ah! A direct descendant of Robin Hood, are we—or merely seeking an ethical justification for our law-breaking?"

"We didn't break the law!" she expostulated, resentfully. "Not on purpose! W-We just sort of . . . twisted it. . . . Anyway," she went on, her confidence waxing with the force of her conviction, "is not Parliament the greatest law-breaker of all—of God's law as well as man's—taking from those with little, to give to those who already have plenty?"

"Though you are obviously unaware of it, my felonious scarecrow," he informed her dryly, "I also pay taxes."

"Not to the cost of the bread on your table, sir, or the very shoes on your feet, or even a solitary ring from your finger! No man wallowing in luxury can know true sacrifice! Do you realise that approximately what you expend on wines in one month, would feed an entire orphanage for a whole year?"

"And with what do you suggest I regale my guests as a reasonable substitute? Holy water?"

Somewhat rashly, Rosalind forgot who she was, where she was, and—what was worse—whom she was addressing, and that her life already hung precariously in the balance, as she shouted in exasperation: "Well, physically it would do them no harm, and spiritually might do them a deal of good!"

A painful silence greeted this, the Duke frowning pensively down at the offending rings adorning his fingers, before casting her a curious sidelong glance.

"You may have a sound argument, Mistress Welsey," he enlightened her, eyes narrowed. "But you overlook a small factor—you are the one on trial here, not I."

Rosalind gasped in dismay, brought up short, face to face with the havoc she had wrought in the space of a few seconds by giving license to that dreadful tongue of hers, which had been her downfall throughout her entire nineteen years, but never as serious as this—at cost of her very

life! She now realised that all was lost—quite, quite lost!
And as her confidence rapidly drained away so did her
colour, turning her as white as the elaborately stuccoed
ceiling at which she now gazed in supplication to heaven,
praying desperately for the miracle to end all miracles
which would save her from the justifiable wrath of the
gentleman before her, to whom she then lowered her
troubled eyes.

"Oh, please, please, forgive me, your Grace!" she
breathed, beside herself with anxiety. "I-I'm sorry—truly,
truly sorry! I swear on my soul, sir, I did not mean to
offend—or criticise you in any way—indeed, I am in no
position to criticise anyone!" She gave licence to a pathetic
little laugh, encouraging him to see the funny side—if
there happened to be one. "I-I pray you won't let this
influence your decision against m-me—or take everything
I said too literally. . . . I know I shouldn't have spoken
out with such conviction—or even spoken at all! Believe
me, my wretched tongue is the bane of my life!"

She looked down at her coat, mortified to find she had
screwed the solitary two buttons off it in her distress—
whilst the Duke continued to survey her, an indescribable
expression registered on his face, experiencing no little
difficulty in reconciling the classic Grecian beauty with the
simple-hearted child obsessed by the primitive urge to
help the needy. Far from being enraged by her outburst,
he was quite astonished—more so to find himself infected
with a germ of admiration. If not actually amused, he
certainly found her a novel diversion from the type of
female he invariably encountered, who suffered not the
slightest compunction in demeaning themselves to curry
his favour—so appealing in their helplessness until challenged by a rival, when they would transform before his

eyes into screeching, savage shrews with claws bared, ready to tear each other to pieces—too absorbed in themselves to spare anyone less fortunate a single thought, let alone hazard their lives for such.

He was smiling pensively to himself, which Rosalind interpreted as favourable, and so breathed easier.

"Your—er—brother," he resumed urbanely, his aristocratic breeding strongly in evidence as he rose, shaking the folds from his coat with a graceful hand, to meander round the room, "—he approves of highwaywomen?"

"N-No, sir—"

"He has survived, I presume?"

"Y-Yes, your Grace—and is greatly improved," she hastened to inform him, eager to please. "I-I really cannot thank you enough, sir, for helping us, and saving Bart's life!"

The Duke halted in his tracks, regarding her askance. "I must differ with you there, child. On the contrary, I am to be censured for his condition, not commended."

"But you could easily have left him on the road to die?"

"True," he concurred, continuing his perambulating. "However, his days may yet be numbered." Sauntering over to the windows, he paused, as if admiring the panoramic view, straining Rosalind's patience to its utmost —but, eventually, he went on. "No doubt you appreciate your precarious position—even so, I shall condescend to make you an offer." Again he hesitated, nervous perspiration breaking out on her forehead, terrified to breathe lest it sway his ultimate decision against her—until he turned, to propose in the same dispassionate tone: "I give you Bart's freedom—in exchange for your own."

The precise wording was unfortunate, and effect dynamic—for in the next instant she was in a panic of supplication at his feet—though for what exactly he was unable to distinguish—playing the devil with his composure.

"Child! What dash't-well ails you?" he demanded, with a grimace as he tried to prise her rigid fingers from his immaculate sleeve.

"I-I d-don't want t-to . . . d-die! I-I'm t-too . . . young . . . to . . . d-die! P-Please . . ." The remainder of her babbled plea was unintelligible as she buried her face in his coat.

"My dear girl," he advised, raising up her woe-begone countenance and compelling her to meet his gaze. "I swear—'tis not my intention that you should."

Rosalind gaped back at him, bewildered. "B-But wh-what else—"

"I mean, that I wish you to remain here under my care—perhaps as companion to my sister, the Lady Isabella. Of course, there is no compulsion, you do have a choice—my offer or the gallows."

"Sir! Y-Your Grace! You cannot know what you are saying!" she gasped, scrambling to her feet from her un-dignified position upon the floor. "Y-You aren't being serious!"

"I assure you, I am not in facetious mood," he returned calmly, reclining against the ornate fireplace of sculptured Italian marble. "And I might add, this decision was not arrived at in the mere tick of a clock. 'Tis the result of a long and onerous cogitation which I found quite fatiguing."

Whilst her host gave licence to a yawn, Rosalind prevaricated, unable to decide if she were more taken aback by the absurdity of the proposal or his lackadaisical manner in proposing it—as if adopting orphans were part of his everyday ritual. In fact, so aghast was she, that she not only forgot her shocking transgression of a moment ago, but allowed her tongue to trangress even further.

"The whole idea is absolutely preposterous!" she ejaculated. "I could never live here! What about her ladyship? What is she going to say to having a nondescript waif— even residing under the same roof, let alone as companion?"

His Grace calmly regaled himself with a glass of Madeira. "I'm afraid her ladyship's sentiments on the matter do not stimulate my interest."

"But you don't realise that I've lived rough and humble for the past four years—and not much better before that! Though educated, I am crude and unpolished! I know as much about drawing-room niceties as I do about tending a . . . a . . . herd of elephants with the distemper! I am hopeless at the keyboard—sir, my playing is simply atrocious—in addition to which, I have difficulty in controlling my tongue—as you've probably gathered—which shatters my conversation! . . . Nor can I manipulate a fan—or swoon to advantage—apart from my gestures which are anything but graceful! And I can't even execute an elegant curtsy, let alone struggle through the minuet! So you must see, your Grace, that I am quite, quite unsuitable!"

As she stood before him heaving for breath, at last able to meet those green mocking eyes, she got the distinct impression he was striving not to smile.

"Rest assured, m' dear," he responded, tongue in cheek —evidently not convinced. "Even I have yet to attain perfection in these arts, but have nevertheless managed along tolerably well thus far"—at which a peculiar sound escaped Rosalind, like a strangled laugh. "This being so," he resumed, mildly curious, "may I enquire the precise nature of the accomplishments you feel competent to boast?"

"I-I speak French and Latin—and can sketch quite well, also paint in oils and water-colours, and weave, sing, sew, cook, ride, fence and—er—shoot."

"An odd curriculum for a convent," he remarked, lazily swishing the wine around in the glass. "You fence well, perchance?"

"Well enough to protect myself!" she replied, a little too forcefully—prompting the heavy lids to rise slowly, revealing a gaze almost sinister.

"Am I to interpret that as some kind of cryptic warning?"

Her eyes wavered and fell, confessing her guilt, as the Duke loomed over her, her gateway to life—or death.

"I give you my word, you will have no need of any such protection from me. It is strongly against even my dubious principles to violate a virgin—that is, if I assume correctly." His manner suddenly changed, as if growing bored with her. "If you have no further objections, you may go. And kindly inform her ladyship that I would see her immediately."

Thankful that the painful interview was over, Rosalind stammered something—she knew not what—and curtsying as best she could, hurriedly withdrew.

It was with grave foreboding that Isabella entered her brother's presence, to quit it ten minutes later in a state of frenzied delight, hastening away to find her newly-acquired companion—utterly mystified (even more so than Rosalind herself) as to why he should suddenly ask her to take Rosalind under her wing and introduce her to the niceties of Society life—apart from bestowing a most generous allowance at her disposal for the cost of a complete wardrobe befitting her new status.

5

As Bart was setting out from Claremont Park to return home three weeks later, in company with Rosalind (who was to make her farewells to his family)—the Duke was arriving at his London town-house in St. James's Square, accompanied by Lord Sevington, and being greeted by a regiment of servants, who leapt forward to relieve him of great-coat, sword and hat before he ascended the stairs to his rooms, with his friend on his heels.

At the fashionable hour of three, the two sat down to dine from a well-laden pedestal table in the Chinese drawing-room where, not surprisingly, everything savoured of the Orient—a thick Chinese carpet, Chinese painted silk embellished with birds and dragons at the windows, Chinese lacquered furniture, Chinese tapestries, and even pagoda lanterns illuminating the room—in addition to the customary candelabra.

Little conversation transpired at first, for as the logs blazed merrily in the hearth, the Viscount mitigated his appetite with a huge slice of choicest beef, and the Duke slaked his thirst with a glass of his best Spanish burgundy.

"How do you propose tracing Sir Roger, Gideon?" asked Lord Sevington, at length, his curiosity overcoming his hunger.

The Duke shrugged indifferently. "I shall make a few tactful enquiries at White's or Almack's—someone is sure to know something. Sixteen years ago," he cast a meaningful look at his friend, "he was residing somewhere in

Sussex, but I never discovered precisely where."

"It's all so deuced confounding!" declared the Viscount, a further helping of beef poised on his fork. "How, in heaven's name, does she come to be languishing in a Wiltshire convent?"

His Grace gestured noncommittally. "What's even more confounding is her mode of life since she left it."

"Yes, b' George—that masquerade was just plain ludicrous!" agreed the other heartily—when a revolting thought struck him. "I say, Gideon!"—he paused until the flunkey had finished replenishing the Duke's glass and moved out of earshot. "That supposed brother of hers— she wasn't his—er—I-I mean, he didn't . . . hum . . . sort of . . . of . . ."

"I shouldn't think so, Chris," responded his Grace with a half-smile. "Incredible though it may seem to you and I, he apparently didn't regard her as a member of the feminine gender."

"Y-You think she is still a—hum—v-virgin, then?" he winced.

" 'S Life, Chris! How your mind does dwell on the sordid," protested the Duke. "If you feel so strongly about it mayhap I should make it my business to find out?"

"Egad, Gideon—not as strongly as that!" exclaimed his friend, shocked, before rapidly diverting his trend of thought. "Am I to understand that you desire her ladyship to be kept in ignorance of it all?" he queried, confidentially.

"For the present, yes. It would serve no purpose to have her unduly alarm the girl."

"And the girl herself—she doesn't suspect?"

The Duke shook his head decisively. "Unless she's a better actress than Kitty Clive, which I doubt."

His lordship grunted. "And Sir Roger? Where d'you think he stands in all this?"

"That, m' good fellow, is what I'm here to find out."

"You have no preconceived ideas?" the Viscount persisted.

"My dear Chris—I do not waste my life in idle speculation. Time alone will assuredly tell."

Lord Sevington seemed prepared to accept this as final and focused his attention on the meal in hand, but anon, cleared his throat—a sure sign that a question of a personal nature was about to follow and which his Grace, thus forewarned, patiently awaited.

"I—er—suppose you realise you will be dragging the proverbial skeleton from the family closet?" he submitted, dubiously.

"I careth not if I evoke an army of the infernal things!" flung back the Duke. "I merely wish to ascertain how I can turn this piece of unbelievable good fortune to my best advantage—mine, mark you! Whatever chances in the process doesn't bother me one jot! There will be misery and heartache—even bloodshed! But if any blood is shed," he added, menacingly, "I assure you, my dear friend, 'twill not be mine."

Silence greeted this as the Duke indicated the cream-and-marzipan gateau, the topic apparently banished from his mind—but it still troubled his lordship.

"No! I refuse to accept it!" he asseverated at this point.

His Grace looked up in surprise. " 'Pon rep, Chris! It isn't as bad as that, surely? Granted, 'tis a trifle overdone, but still quite edible. Try the veal if the ham isn't to your liking."

"Th-the ham is excellent, thank you," faltered the other, puzzled.

"Then what, may I ask, do you refuse to accept so dogmatically?"

"Sir Roger!" obliged his lordship, fervently. "I simply cannot believe he had any hand in disowning his daughter in such a fashion. Only met him the once, mind you, but he was a decent fellow—wouldn't do anything underhanded! Swear an oath on it!"

"Which, my good comrade, I'd be the last to deny," supported the Duke, amiably. "But I was under the impression you regarded her origin as somewhat doubtful?"

"Oh . . . hum . . . quite," he agreed, shamefacedly, trying to stare the pattern off his plate before flashing the Duke a guilty look to venture, with the utmost caution: "Has it perhaps occurred to you, Gideon, that she could possibly be of—hum—even better stock than Tremayne, but—er—on the wrong side of the —hum—" He broke off, aware that the Duke had perceived his meaning.

"For instance, Claremont stock?"

The Viscount rose hurriedly to his feet. "I-I'm sorry, Gideon. I apologise most profoundly—I had no right to infer such a thing. . . . Y-You may have satisfaction when and where you will—"

"Plague take ye, Chris! Sit down!" the Duke besought him, striving to keep his countenance. "You know well enough I'd never accept a challenge from you—and don't be such a confounded hypocrite! You are bursting to know whether she is or not—it's blazing in your face! Be brave —admit it!"

"We . . . ll," prevaricated his lordship, as the Duke rose from the table, glass in hand, to stroll across to the fireplace.

"Had she been a year or two younger, I confess, I should have harboured similar doubts. However, as I first

—shall we say—compromised Eugenia less than seventeen years ago, and the girl is now nineteen, your supposition can hardly be true. I trust that satisfies your morbid curiosity?"

His lordship resumed his seat, mumuring something incoherent.

" 'Tis p'raps as well for her sake," went on the Duke, a caustic edge to his voice. "I should say she already has ample bad blood in her veins without the addition of mine."

Able to think of no apt response, and finding the depressing turn of conversation not at all to his taste, Lord Sevington channelled the discourse back to Sir Roger.

"If Sir Roger still resides in Sussex, Gideon, you—hum —intend journeying hence very soon?"

"Probably sometime next week," he replied, casually.

"You don't think it will prove a waste of time?"

"On the contrary, m' dear fellow—I shall benefit prodigiously from the exercise! Don't get enough of it, y' know."

"I refer to Sir Roger," pointed out the other, with a frown of irritation. "Should you be fortunate enough to find him, I doubt very much if he'll know ought of the girl's existence."

"However," responded the Duke, relinquishing his glass to adjourn to his rooms and embark upon his lengthy toilet—his valet suddenly materialising at his elbow—"he may know something of his wife's, which information I also go to ferret out."

"My guess is," went on the Viscount, rising instinctively to take his leave, "that someone else fathered her, and Eugenia put her in the convent to avoid a scandal."

"Eugenia?" ejaculated the Duke with a laugh. "My dear

Chris—she positively thrives on't!" He paused by the door to regard the Viscount shrewdly. "You have no need to fret, my friend. I do not intend throwing discretion to the winds and jumping in with both feet without first removing my boots."

"But being a gentleman of honour, I fail to see how you can expect him to throw any light on the matter," pursued his lordship, dogging the Duke's steps to the foot of the stairs—where his Grace meandered to a halt.

"I expect nought of no one—never have and never shall —thus I manage to avoid disappointment." He seemed about to mount the stairs when he paused, an enigmatic smile playing about his lips. "Anyway, dear Chris, you forget—I merely plan to make a long-delayed social call upon Sir Roger, to hazard the lay o' the land. Should he happen to let fall some chance information—assuming I find him—then 'twill be to my added benefit, will't not?"

And so saying, he bid his lordship a pleasant adieu, before ascending the stairs to prepare for an evening at his club—leaving an extremely thoughtful Viscount to wend his way home.

6

As the duke had foreseen, he experienced little difficulty in acquiring the information he sought, being fortunate to encounter a certain elderly member of his club who had known Sir Roger many years ago, and who revealed that his estate lay somewhere betwixt Horsham and Wisborough Green, but nurtured some doubt if he would still be alive as he had never enjoyed robust health. Upon the Duke extending his enquiry to the whereabouts of Lady Tremayne, the gentleman regretfully knew nought of her —save that she had caused her husband acute embarrassment during their early married life, due to which Sir Roger had been obliged to retire from Society to a life of seclusion.

And so, the Duke undertook his journey to Sussex upon the following Monday in company with his valet, who was astounded at his master's predilection to travel on horse, and after a mile or so expected him to relinquish the steed in favour of a hired chaise. But Paul was filled with pride when they eventually reached Horsham without a single oath escaping the Duke's lips.

It was noon when his Grace trotted blithely into the rural town where he stopped awhile to refresh his horse and slake his thirst at a local inn, while Paul busied himself making enquiries regarding their destination.

At length, master and servant remounted and cantered out of the town, setting their course for Wisborough Green, as according to an ale-bibbing rustic seated upon a bench outside the inn, Sir Roger's estate lay barely five miles farther that way.

Therefore, it was not long before what appeared to be a splendid building in grounds of goodly size was sighted in an outlandish spot with nothing else in view. Of course his Grace had yet to discover if this were the abode of the Tremaynes, and so, urged his horse into a gallop until the estate was reached, when he slowed to a trot, passing through the rusty wrought iron gates and up the drive to halt at the door. Here, he sat awhile, critically surveying the exterior, to find that at this range the building was not nearly so impressive, having sadly deteriorated over the years, probably due to financial difficulties. Neither did there appear to be any sign of life as he dismounted and approached the forbidding door to beat a loud tattoo with his riding crop. Twice was this medium plied thus, sending a sinister resounding clamour throughout the vast empty house. Suddenly, on raising his head to glance over the facade, his eye was arrested by a weatherbeaten inscription hanging over the door which read, in faded gold characters: 'Tremayne Grange.'

Howbeit, he was beginning to think he had indeed come on a fool's errand when the sound of shambling, somewhat reticent footsteps responded to the call. And after rusty bolts were drawn (with no little bother and prodigious noise) the heavy door groaned ajar to reveal an aged man-servant, who was not given an opportunity to make utterance before the Duke demanded, with hauteur: "Sir Roger Tremayne still reside here?"

The menial eyed the distinguished visitor from head to foot, a look of suspicious enquiry on his wrinkled face.

"Y-Yes, y'r honour," he replied, when satisfied with the

Duke's appearance, bowing as low as his ancient bones would permit.

"He is within?"

"Y-Yes—but whom—"

The Duke advanced over the threshold, gesturing servant and protests aside with a casual wave.

"Kindly inform your master that the Duke of Delvray desires speech with him." And so saying, delivered hat and riding-crop into the other's care.

At first the servant gasped, gaped, then stammered to an accompaniment of bows: "M-Most certainly, y'r Grace! A-At once, y'r G-Grace!" and so, hobbled away to execute the command.

Whilst he was gone, the Duke indulged in a pinch of snuff, observing with an air of disrelish, the musty degenerate interior of what had once been a house of the first consequence, but was now laid low with threadbare carpets, sparse warped furniture, and tapestries performing a miracle by simply remaining intact. Dust lay everywhere, inducing him to brush a hand down the fine blue broadcloth of his coat, a little too emphatically for the sole purpose of removing snuff.

Eventually, the shuffling feet (with more urgency in their tread) heralded the menial's return who, with enormous ceremony, then conducted the Duke to the rear of the house and into a moderately sized, comfortably furnished study, which stood at odds with the rest of the dwelling. The mild surprise which crossed his face did not go unremarked by his host who at once made to greet him, laying spectacles aside—a tall gaunt elderly gentleman, with shoulders hunched as if permanently chilled, and a face bearing a shadowy resemblance of its former handsomeness, topped by a brown scratch-wig and a frayed red woollen cap.

"Good-day, Sir Roger," the Duke ventured. "I trust you will forgive the intrusion, and that I find you well?"

"Good-day, indeed, your Grace," returned the other, cordially. "I deem myself honoured that you should inconvenience your noble person by undertaking such a tiresome journey on my behalf. Pray be seated! My health, of course, is not what it once was, but I suppose one cannot complain at my age"—adding on afterthought, "I crave forgiveness for receiving you in such deficient surroundings but I inhabit only this solitary wing—and the rest of the house is closed off and never used, you understand?"

The Duke smiled his understanding and disposed himself with ease in the chair indicated by his host.

Sir Roger, aged though he may be, knew well enough that this unexpected visit of his Grace could be only to rake up the dismal past, but even so, concealed his curiosity and perturbation admirably, beneath a veneer of good manners as he proffered a limited choice of wines for his guest's refreshment. Selecting the most palatable, the Duke stealthily regarded his host awhile, before permitting his eyes to wander at will.

Arrayed round the walls was an incalculable number of books, including the entire literary works of the essayist of the day—Dr. Samuel Johnson, whom Sir Roger evidently held in great esteem as a copy of the noteworthy gentleman's most recent success lay open upon the walnut writing desk. It was with an imperceptible tremor that Sir Roger presented the wine to his visitor, but which did not go unnoticed by his Grace—who obligingly accredited the weakness to his host's premature old age, rather than any effect he personally might engender.

As the two were not well acquainted, it was with some caution that they conversationally probed their way with small-talk, until the acute agitation of Sir Roger became so pronounced that his guest capitulated and directed the discourse round to the reason for his visit—as usual, not mincing the matter.

"Doubtless, you appreciate, Sir Roger, that I did not journey thither solely to partake of the Sussex air, however beneficial it may be," he informed his host with languid affability. "Therefore, I shall without further ado, embark upon the imperative business quite recently come to light, of which—as you will anon surely agree—I deemed it my responsibility to apprise you as soon as my multitudinous duties would allow."

In reply, the other said nothing, but gave a wan smile of comprehension, relieved at getting to the crux of the matter, while the Duke—savouring the moment—took a last lingering sip of wine, rendered his person more comfortable, then began.

"As you may already suspect, sir, the whole affair centres round your—er—wife." The word 'wife', being flavoured with ill-suppressed sarcasm, caused Sir Roger to wince visibly.

"I trust you are able to justify resurrecting a period of my life which brings nought but bitter anguish?"

"Perchance it evades your memory, sir, but I happen to number one of your wife's earliest conquests and find little pleasure in reanimating the lamentable past without excellent cause."

Sir Roger nodded his sympathetic appreciation, and lowered his head to murmur: "You may speak freely, your Grace."

An element of relief flashed across the Duke's face.

"This question may seem of a personal nature, but I assure you, is of the utmost importance." He paused, glancing warily at his host whose attention was still on his be-slippered feet. "Has your wife, to your knowledge, ever borne any offspring, legitimate or otherwise?"

The bewigged head rose abruptly. "Really, sir! I cannot see—"

"I repeat, Sir Roger—the question is vital!"

The old man stared in pained bewilderment. "A-Am I to understand that my wife—though rather wayward—mentioned nought of our ch-child?"

"Well," returned the Duke gently, schooling his feelings, "as I was unaware at the time that she even possessed a husband, a child would have proved a trifle awkward to explain, would it not?"

"Oh—er—quite so," he concurred, comprehending his error, and for a while seemed to argue within himself, plucking nervously at the worn brown woollen robe covering his knees, then suddenly come to a decision. "Perhaps it would be better if . . . W-Would you care to hear the whole sad tale?"

The Duke smiled in patient acknowledgment—but his curiosity to the fore, as Sir Roger rose to replenish their glasses.

"Our child—a girl—was born nineteen years ago past August—the fifth, to be precise. It was the most wonderful experience of my life! She was a beautiful child, but with each new day grew even more so, with cheeks like roses, eyes as blue as the heavens, and the loveliest curls one could wish to see." Here, Sir Roger thought it advisable to reseat himself. "Those were happy days indeed, but, strangely, I sensed that no human being was destined to be so happy—possibly because Eugenia's former affection for Rosalind—" the Duke's interest quickened at the name "—slowly changed to indifference and finally resentment. This may have been due to jealousy of the child's exceptional beauty, I cannot tell. However, my ominous feeling proved true. It was during the month of October, when my child was in her third year, that the terrible tragedy occurred."

Sir Roger took a large gulp of port, as if to fortify himself for what was to come, conscious of his guest's undivided attention.

"Eugenia developed an urge to visit friends in Bath and was most anxious to take Rosalind to let them see how well the child was progressing. So, on October 6th, the most precious possession in my life departed. Little did I realise at the time, that I w-was never ag-again t-to . . . see . . . her." An inflection in his voice prompted further recourse to his glass. "On October 28th, my wife returned alone, with the dreadful news of Rosalind's accident. Seemingly she had run unwittingly into the roadway in pursuit of a small dog, to be taken unawares by an oncoming coach, and tr-trampled to d-death 'neath . . . the h-horses' . . . h-hooves . . ."

This last stammered revelation shot his listener's dark brows up in some astonishment, which passed unseen by Sir Roger, who sat rapt in despair awhile, before rallying himself sufficiently to add: "H-Her small body was s-so badly m-marred, it was essential that she be in-interred immediately, w-with the . . . brief . . . est . . . of f-for . . . mal . . . ities."

It proved too much for Sir Roger, who broke down completely at this point, giving licence to the tears which rained upon his hands—while the Duke's subtle mind raced on ahead, fitting together the whole malicious scheme of that accursed woman. Outwardly, he affected his customary impassiveness, but his eyes blazed and, as usual, one beringed hand gripped the chair-arm.

He traced his memory back to that wretched period in his life, deducing that it was at this same time he had held Eugenia's warm pulsating body close to his heart, and found it impossible to credit that during those rapturous moments she had been callously plotting to dispose of her own flesh and blood, ensuring that nought stood betwixt her and her desires—for, as the child matured, not only would she prove an obstacle, but a formidable rival. How he had underrated this Jezebel—this female Satan whom he had, in his mad impetuous youth, almost vowed to love and cherish till death. He had been her slave—had paid homage at her feet—had loved her body and soul to the point of madness, with a holy sacrificial love which had suddenly gone sour, turning to hate—an intense hate! And this hatred he had nurtured over the years until it now consumed his entire being, crying out for vengeance—which he now saw within his grasp.

But this compared little to the burden Sir Roger had borne. It was a miracle how his frail form had survived the past agonising years in bondage to this witch, who had drained him of all his resources, then deserted him in favour of a wealthier bird with finer plumage. This inspired the Duke to rise and place a firm but comforting hand upon his host's heaving shoulder, to administer more wine to his quivering lips. Sir Roger took three lingering sips ere he achieved some self-control, but his voice still shook.

"I-It was my dearest wish that her body be brought here to be placed in the family vault where she truly belongs, but the very idea filled Eugenia with revulsion."

The Duke sneered to himself as he replaced the glass by Sir Roger's elbow and assumed a pose by the window, silently absorbing this new information, whilst enjoying the impressive view of rural Sussex. He allowed several minutes to lapse before resuming.

"You may think me a trifle unfeeling, Sir Roger, but circumstances beyond my control compel me to pursue this nauseating business to the bitter end."

Sir Roger looked understandably puzzled.

"I come as an angel of good tidings," went on the Duke, in lighter vein, perusing the divers volumes upon the shelves beside him, with an air of idle interest. "A role which does not suit me well, I might add. Even so, what would you say if I were to tell you that once again you have been the victim of your dear Eugenia's diabolical deceit—by pronouncing the entire account you have just honoured me with, nought but a farrago of lies?"

The old man's eyes bulged from his head as if stricken with a seizure, and the oak arms of his chair creaked beneath the rigid grip of his prominently veined hands. Thus he sat, like a marble statue, until the colour gradually crept back into his lips, as he tried to fashion them into words.

"W-With all respect, your G-Grace," he gasped weakly, "m-my wine must not ag-agree with y-you."

"I was never more sober in my life," his guest responded calmly.

Sir Roger eagerly drained his glass, his eyes never leaving the Duke's face.

"I-I trust you are able to cor-corroborate your statement?"

His Grace sauntered back to his chair and, leaning forward, gazed directly into the other's dumbfounded face.

"Would it be proof enough if I were to present you with your daughter Rosalind in the flesh?"

Sir Roger blanched. "H-How c-can such a th-thing be p-possible . . . b-by what foul means . . . black magic or w-witchcraft?"

"Neither," replied the Duke, lounging back in his chair, the better to contemplate his fingernails, as the clock ticked monotonously on, quite unimpressed by the drama. "For the past sixteen years she has been languishing in a convent."

Once again was Sir Roger bereft of words. "A-A con-convent! B-But where? H-How?"

"In Wiltshire," supplied his Grace, deeming it politic to make no mention of Rosalind's association with the dubious Bart. "But how?—there you have me, and hence the reason for my visit."

"Y-You think Eugenia put her in the convent?"

The Duke shrugged. "It is possible, but highly improbable. If Eugenia wanted rid of her daughter she wouldn't leave the job half done. I believe she hired an assassin whose courage failed at the vital moment and panicked, leaving the child on the steps of the convent, hoping her identity would never be discovered."

"But it . . . it . . ." Sir Roger broke off, completely at a loss. "P-Pray give me a moment . . . my aging mind needs time to grasp it."

"Your wife gave you no cause to doubt her story?" queried the Duke at length, whilst his host sat with a hand adhered to his forehead, struggling to digest the startling information.

"None whatever, your Grace! In fact, she was most distressed at the time, I remember quite well . . . er—am I permitted to ask how you know all this?"

The Duke paused, briefly debating how much to divulge. "I acquired my information from a most reliable source, sir—from Rosalind herself whom I—"

"What!" burst out Sir Roger, jumping up with surprising agility to hover in front of his guest, wringing his hands, a look of ineffable joy on his wrinkled face. "Y-You have actually spoken with her? I-It is really she—there can be no doubt?"

"None at all!"

"Wh-where is she now? You have brought her? She is here?"

"I'm afraid not," confessed the Duke, ruefully. "You'll appreciate, sir, I had first of all to establish her background—"

"But she is safe?" intersected his host, anxiously.

"Quite safe, I assure you—"

"You are certain? An-and well—she is well?"

"Extremely well."

"P-Pray forgive me, your Grace," gasped the old man. "I-I am quite overcome, and have so much to ask. . . ."

Sir Roger limped about the room in evidence of the injury sustained from a riding accident in his youth, and which became more pronounced under stress.

"I understand perfectly, Sir Roger, and will endeavour to answer your questions to the best of my ability. I did take it upon myself to pay a call at the convent," went on the Duke, striving to recapture the elusive name, "the Convent of the—er—Blessed something—hoping to glean further information—"

"And you discovered?" prompted the other, agog.

"Nothing, alas! All they knew was what the child herself had told them—that her name was Rosalind and her mother had left her with a stranger, who had abandoned her."

"I-I just can't believe it!" gasped Sir Roger for the tenth time, still stupefied by the news, and like to be for some months to come. "It-it's like some fantastic dream come true!" He sat down again to stare intently at the Duke. "You must tell me everything, your Grace—exactly how this miracle came about!"

"Well, by some uncanny twist of fate, I found her destitute en route to my estate in Wiltshire—she having escaped from her 'convent prison', as she put it. She was in a rather bedraggled condition, to say the least, but even so, I was immediately struck by her unmistakable likeness to your wife, and conveyed her to my residence to have her taken care of. At present, she is acting as a bewildered companion to my sister, the Lady Isabella."

His Grace saw no point in alarming his host unduly by relating the true course of events.

"Poor child!" exclaimed the other, deeply moved. "She must have been sadly overwrought . . . and you say she was just wandering alone—you discovered her quite by chance?"

"Er—quite—or rather, she discovered me," replied the Duke, evasively.

"Discovered you? Y-You mean, she approached you?" pressed Sir Roger, eyebrows raised, apparently not going to be satisfied with this hazy reply. "To perhaps seek advice?"

"True, she did stop me to make a request," responded his guest, tongue in cheek. "But whether she sought advice or no, she was certainly given some."

"Admirable!" he approved, to the Duke's amusement. "I'm sure she stood in need of it." He paused, stroking his smoothly-shaven chin. "But to meet you of all people . . . has indeed been the hand of Providence. Permit me to say here and now, your Grace, that I cannot sufficiently express my gratitude for all you have done, and the way you have inconvenienced yourself on my daughter's behalf. I dread to think what might have chanced had she fallen into other hands."

His Grace accepted the embarrassing gratitude of his host without a single pang of conscience, idly pondering how his intimates would have differed with this opinion— justifiably so.

Anticipating Sir Roger's next question, he forestalled him.

"When you meet her, you will understand how I recognised her instantly. There is no disputing she's Eugenia's child."

"There's a strong resemblance?"

"In looks, yes—but there, I'm relieved to say, the resemblance ends. Their natures are as far apart as heaven and the—er—other place. She reveres me like an archbishop and overwhelms me with gratitude over the merest trifles, which, you must agree, does not identify with Eugenia."

"Indeed not!" accorded his host, fervently.

The Duke, having arrived at the crucial question, frowned, meditating how best to deliver it for casual effect.

"I presume you have not seen her recently, Sir Roger?" he probed, at length.

"No—not for well over three years—nor wish to!"

"Then you know nought of her whereabouts?"

Sir Roger shook his head. "She was still in France until a few months ago, as I heard from a trustworthy party that she had been sent to the Bastille, of all places, on a *lettre de cachet*, but had since managed to secure her release with the aid of an influential friend—probably the devil himself! What she's done to the poor wretch she ran off with, I cannot bear to think."

"I imagine he'll have learnt his lesson by now, like the rest of us," observed the Duke, placidly—though inwardly rankled at losing such a valuable opportunity to acquire his vengeance during his sojourn in Paris—no doubt when Eugenia had been incarcerated in the Bastille.

"Yes, b' George!" seconded the other, passionately roused. "And a bitter one too, I warrant! If she ever does come back I'll teach her something she won't forget overnight!" Sudden appreciation of his wife's vile deception surged through him like a maelstrom, and his voice—beginning a low menacing growl—rose to a powerful crescendo, almost hysterical. "I could kill her! I could kill her! Better still, I *will* kill her!"—his clenched fist pounding the table, making bottles and wineglasses jangle and dance on the polished surface.

"Sir Roger," came the Duke's voice, little more than a whisper but effectively quelling the savage outburst which had fallen like a curse on the old man. "Killing is too good for her. She should be made to suffer as you have suffered and if you leave everything to me, I promise you she will."

Sir Roger swiftly regained his composure and sat up, straightening his wig with a mumbled apology, turning to regard his guest in anxious enquiry.

"Y-You have something in mind, perchance?"

"Perchance I have," returned the Duke cryptically, contemplating the dust on his left boot. "I merely plan to bait my trap, then sit back and wait. Her jealousy and greed are sure to land her in it eventually, if I wait long enough—having waited sixteen years already, I am not feverish with impatience."

"And with what, precisely, do you intend baiting your trap?" queried Sir Roger, sceptically. "Half your fortune?"

"Not with what, sir—but with whom," amended the Duke significantly, to await the outburst which would assuredly follow—which was not long.

"You plan to use my daughter as a decoy, sirrah?" exploded his host.

"I had not intended putting it quite so bluntly—but I must confess, my sole interest in her is that she can further my ambition." And as the other looked about to have an apoplexy, he hastened to add: "Do not distress yourself, Sir Roger. I assure you, I have the purest intentions towards your daughter which—I appreciate—stand at odds with my repute. I merely wish to patronise her, nothing more."

A stunned silence met this disclosure.

"P-Patronise her?" faltered Sir Roger. "I d-don't quite follow."

"Permit me to elucidate," besought the Duke, reclining in his chair—more at ease now that the awkward moment was passed. "I propose—with your approbation of course —to cultivate her to the pinnacle of perfection, drape her in silks, satins and jewels—then present her to the world with all the dignity and splendour at my command. What woman as insanely jealous as your wife could endure to see her bewitching daughter resurrected to become the toast of London—the darling of Society—and, what is more, under my patronage?"

Sir Roger gaped yet again at his guest—not a sign of anger in evidence. "Y-You would do all that for my daughter?" he stammered, incredulously.

"To restore my wounded pride and family honour—yes! I do not tolerate lightly, being made a fool of, which your wife will learn one day to her bitter regret."

"Th-then you are in deadly earnest? You mean what you say?"

His Grace inclined his head as Sir Roger churned the proposal over in his mind, nibbling the nail of his right thumb.

"I must say, that as I now have a daughter again it would give me no greater pleasure than to see her well established," he confessed eventually, entering into the scheme with enthusiasm. "And as I have neither the influence nor the wherewithal to do it—why not? Why not indeed?" Rising promptly afoot, he seized the Duke's hand to pump it up and down. "I agree! I agree most heartily, your Grace! My child cannot fail to be highly delighted at the prospect. I bestow upon you full power of guardianship over her! I trust you with the care and protection of my most treasured possession! I beg, sir, that you will honour my trust, as a gentleman."

"You may rest assured, Sir Roger, I shall watch over her like a guardian angel," replied the Duke, likewise rising to seal the agreement. "Naturally, I shall not hesitate to consult you with any vital decisions which may have to be made on her behalf—and my house will be ever open for you to visit her whene'er you wish."

Sir Roger could scarce believe that within the space of a few hours his beloved daughter was not only returned from the dead, but having a brilliant future planned. She could not help but make a splendid match if all his guest said were true! Tears—now of joy—ran down his cheeks, partly at his own and Rosalind's extraordinary good fortune, and partly at thoughts of the agony of remorse in store for his wife.

Meanwhile, his guest surveyed him through his long black lashes, smiling cryptically to himself—a smile of supreme satisfaction that the day's events had turned out so well, and his campaign of vengeance was already under way.

7

Never had there been such commotion as there was at Claremont Park on this October day, the time having drawn nigh for the departure to London of Isabella and Rosalind. An impressive calvacade of conveyances (excelled only by the Duke himself) monopolised the driveway—the amount of baggage piled thereon enough to accommodate an army.

But this external hubbub created by the servants plying back and forth like a colony of ants was but a murmur compared to the din inside. Her ladyship's delicate throat was positively hoarse through giving orders and now even she agreed that there could not be a single item overlooked. Already she felt quite exhausted and the long journey had not yet begun. Consequently, when she and Rosalind eventually climbed into the coach it was with no little relief—though more at being disburdened of her brother who had left two days earlier with Paul in the light travelling carriage, for—as she confided to Rosalind —'Gideon never knew when to maintain a proper silence!' And having a sizeable retinue they had no need to fear for their personal safety. Indeed, Isabella was in whoops of delight at having her freedom en route, and was equally looking forward to staying with her aunt, as even this punctilious person was 'loose on the reins' compared with Gideon—and in London of all places!

However, by the time they had endured two full days' travelling their enthusiasm was beginning to wilt, as de-

spite the modern well-sprung vehicle, their bones felt
shook to pieces, and her ladyship—suffering with the
headache and having frequent recourse to her vinaigrette
—felt ready for her bed shortly after dinner that day. And
so, three miles out of Reading they spied an inn and
decided to secure rooms for the night, only too thankful
to quit the road although it promised another two hours'
daylight—but, alas, found all the best rooms at 'The Gay
Cavalier' already bespoken and themselves obliged to
share the last room available (but with the most inspiring
view, mine host reiterated) as it was the only reputable
inn this side of the town. This meant that the major part
of my lady's retinue had to seek shelter at the rather
boisterous 'Green Unicorn' farther down the road.

The overcrowded inn, however, was found to have at
least one compensation in the shape of a young beau
burdened with the name of Lord Algernon Enwright, with
whom my lady was already on acquaintance and who
cordially invited them to dine with him and his party.
Rosalind doubted the propriety of accepting until she discovered that the party embraced his lordship's rheumaticky
aunt.

The following morning saw Isabella and Rosalind gathering themselves together at an early hour in the hope of
seeing London by noon that day. Lord Enwright wanted
to escort them as he was headed (like everyone else) for
London too, but was beholden to wait upon his aunt, who
never rose before eleven.

Howbeit, it was almost three o'clock when Rosalind
got her first glimpse of the capital, and almost four by the
time the coachman had threaded his way through the
riotous streets to Cavendish Square where the Duke's
paternal aunt, the Countess de Toulière resided, who was

to assume the entire responsibility of Rosalind's introduction to Society.

At last, they rumbled to a halt at the door, to be joyfully welcomed by the Countess herself—small and plump of stature, with blue eyes adance in a rosy face which was supported by rippling chins—who ushered them indoors like a mother hen with her chicks.

"So! This is Rosalind!" she declared, excitedly, before Isabella could say anything. "Exquisite, my dear! Simply exquisite! I vow Gideon's opinion was always to be relied upon! Dear child," she went on, "I do hope you will enjoy your stay and grow to love London as much as I."

"Oh—I love it already!" responded Rosalind, breathlessly.

"You shall call me Aunt Gertrude, as my own niece does," she chatted on in ever-mounting pitch, "then we shall all deal famously together!" And with that, she hugged and kissed Isabella who was beginning to feel left out of it all. "I must commend you, Isabella, on your excellent results. I understand from Gideon that Rosalind was quite provincial?" She paused to beam admiration upon Rosalind again. "I vow the whole *Beau Monde* is agog to see this fair paragon shrouded in mystery," she continued without a breath. "Having materialised out of the blue, so to speak—and patronised by not only *a* Duke, but *the* Duke! I declare the tongues are still wagging over your own coming out last year! What an occasion!" And so she rattled on, with all the current gossip and scandal in London.

Following her arrival, Rosalind wsa granted two days to settle in ere Aunt Gertrude set to work to mould her to perfection. The Countess's hands shot up in horror at a sample of her dancing, and promptly reserved two hours each day for the remaining weeks with Monsieur Arnaud, the most eminent dancing master in the city. And as she also handled her fan rather awkwardly, half an hour per day was set aside to achieve proficiency in this—and so it went on—Isabella assisting all she could and proving as harsh a critic as her aunt.

Consequently, by the end of the month a very different Rosalind emerged—graceful, sublime and accomplished in every detail. Her curtsy was a joy to behold, and her manipulation of a fan a masterpiece of dexterity which brought tears of admiration to the Countess's eyes. With Isabella, she was permitted to attend museums, art galleries, exhibitions, and promenade through the parks at the fashionable hour. Everywhere they went, heads turned, pencilled brows were raised, and surreptitious whispers heard, which Rosalind enjoyed immensely.

Each time they sallied forth Isabella's eager eye was on the alert for Lord Sevington, but this pleasure was constantly denied her, until one day her aunt threw her into raptures by announcing that her brother and Lord Sevington had accepted her invitation to take tea with them the following Monday—with an extra special guest.

However, tea was not the sole reason for the countess's invitation to her nephew, for not only did she have something of an extremely urgent and delicate nature to impart, but desired him to see the change in his ward and solicit his good opinion of the ballroom—the decoration of which was now well under way as the actual ball was to take place on Friday of that week, after the Court presentation. Over eight hundred hand-picked guests had been invited, which would no doubt prove a frightful 'squeeze' should they all feel inclined to dance at once, but of a surety, a fair proportion of the gentlemen would spend a deal of time—if not the entire evening—at the card tables.

But strange as it may seem, by Monday Rosalind was experiencing little enthusiasm for the grand occasion. Instead, she felt a peculiar sensation—something she had certainly never felt before. She suffered no physical pain, or felt ill—though it did seem like a kind of sickness at times—but found herself perpetually daydreaming, her thoughts much preoccupied by a certain gentleman whom, she was deeply conscious, she ought not to think such thoughts about, yet was unable (and admittedly unwilling) to banish them from her head. Sometimes they really were quite shocking—when she would redden with guilt, believing them to be written openly on her forehead for all to read—at the same time fervently thanking heaven that the object of her dreams was wholly unaware of the romantic role he played in her fanciful notions—and prayed he would remain so.

True to their word, the Duke and Viscount established themselves in the Countess's drawing-room at five o'clock that day for their tea engagement, his Grace pleasantly surprised at the improvement in his ward upon which he at once complimented his aunt. Five minutes later the clatter of hooves and rumble of wheels heralded the Countess's 'special' guest, being—to Rosalind's wild delight—her father, Sir Roger, with whom she had swiftly developed an intimate relationship during his stay at Claremont Park, despite the incongruous circumstances surrounding her mother—whose name she had soon learned never to mention. The Countess had sent her own coach and four to convey Sir Roger hither as a treat for him and his daughter due to his inability to attend the ball —the true reason being that he was loth to risk reminding anyone with a retentive memory, of Rosalind's unfortunate connection with her mother.

Greetings over, the Countess decided that tea would be served without any ado, and considered it proper for Rosalind to perform this office, thereby gaining experience in English Society's most important ritual. Yielding gracefully, her pupil discharged the duty with admirable finesse —until she arrived at the Duke. All may have been well had she not allowed her eyes to wander to his—but she did, and so followed disaster. For some odd reason her hand shook uncontrollably, the cup tottering precariously on the saucer ere it descended into his lap, showering contents over his claret velvet coat. Rosalind found her composure shattered and panic ensued, amidst a flurry of apologies.

"I-I'm dreadfully sorry, y-your Grace," she stammered for the sixth time in as many seconds. "P-Please don't be upset. . . . I shall have it c-cleaned up in a trice." And whipping forth her flimsy handkerchief, proceeded to rub vigorously at the offending tea-stains, much to the Duke's consternation, who hastily clapped hand to eyes at the excruciating sight of the bald patches emerging in his costly velvet. How the incident passed unnoticed by Aunt Gertrude was nothing short of a miracle, but fortunately she was in close conversation with Sir Roger otherwise the fat would indeed have been in the fire.

Rosalind glanced anxiously round, relieved to see the Countess and her father engrossed in their discourse and Isabella and the Viscount engrossed in each other—even the clattering tea-cups had failed to rouse any response from that quarter.

"If your aunt discovers this she will make me serve tea every hour for a week!" she whispered cautiously to the

Duke, as she quickly furnished him with another cup and deposited it in front of him with infinite care—nurturing a strange fancy that he was struggling not to smile. "I seem to get deeper in your debt every time we meet. How can I ever hope to repay you?"

"Fret not, Melpomene," he returned, his mocking tone belying a veiled threat. "I've no doubt you will—sooner than you think."

She was about to enquire the meaning behind this cryptic warning when the Countess broke in, expressing her regrets to Rosalind at monopolising her father's attention, and suggesting she entertain him while she acquired the Duke's worthy opinion of the ballroom.

The Countess then conducted the Duke—not immediately to the ballroom, but to a room up another two flights of stairs at the rear of the house—a precaution lest their intimate conversation be overheard. The room had been her late husband's study and was still comfortably furnished as such.

Whilst the Duke languidly bestowed himself in a chair by the fire, his handsome face registering bored resignation (convinced that his aunt had nought more urgent to confide than the colour of her undergarments for the ball), the Countess closed the door and crossed with a swish of her purple satin gown to the japanned cabinet by the window, where she measured out a large brandy. This, she delivered into the Duke's astonished hands before establishing herself opposite him, arraying her voluminous skirt about her with ceremony. She then fixed him with a piercing eye, her usually cheerful lips set most forbiddingly whilst her ample bosom heaved spasmodically, and her fingers twiddled in her lap.

"I gather 'tis your present custom to serve brandy with

tea and chocolate cake?" he enquired satirically—adding: "'Pon rep, Aunt! You seem all afidget! Methinks you need the brandy."

The Countess rejected the glass with a gesture of disdain, pointing out that she retained it for medicinal purposes only, and that (as he was already availing himself of it) she had given it him as restorative—not refreshment!

"Faith, you mean what you have to divulge is even more astounding than 'Bella ogling Chris?"

She ignored his irony. "It most certainly is!" she declared roundly. "It could utterly ruin your plans—my plans—everything!"

He did not respond but calmly sipped the brandy, patiently awaiting her vastly magnified revelation.

"Of course, being a mere male," she chided him, "I doubt very much if you will have even noticed it! To me, however, it is blatantly obvious that your ward—"

"Plague on't" broke in her nephew, stifling a yawn. "Don't tell me she still hasn't mastered the confounded minuet?"

"Gideon! Will you be serious and please listen! It is no joking matter."

"I hear and obey," he replied, assuming a solemn visage. "Speak—I am all agog!"

The Countess frowned disapprovingly. With his nose stuck in the brandy-glass he seemed to be anything but agog.

"I repeat, Nephew, to me it is perfectly obvious that your ward is head-over-heels in love!"

His Grace coughed, spluttered, but rapidly recovered himself to stare incredulously at his aunt, all traces of humour wiped clean from his face.

"We are discussing Miss Tremayne, are we not?"

"We are," seconded the Countess firmly. "Rosalind, your ward, my protégée."

"You are absolutely certain of this, Aunt?"

"With my wealth of experience, Gideon, how could I be mistaken?"

"Damnation!" he swore under his breath.

An interminable silence greeted the disclosure, it having indeed given the Duke food for thought, whilst his aunt tugged irritably at the ribbons of her French cap tied 'neath her triple chins, as she argued with herself how best to follow up the startling news.

"Have you any idea whom the man might be, Gideon?" she probed at length, doubting the wisdom of interrupting his thoughts. "I have made my own deductions, of course, but so far haven't arrived at any reasonable conclusion. Only yesterday I took it upon myself to question Isabella —er—circumspectly, you understand," she hastened to point out, "and apparently the only gentleman Rosalind has spent any time with in London is a certain Lord Algernon Enwright, who," grimaced the Countess, "I made it my business to find out and am horrified to inform you—has traces of insanity in his family and is up to his neck in debt!"

Still no response was forthcoming.

"However—though I see little to choose 'twixt the two— Isabella also mentioned some rather peculiar person named Bart." She shuddered with disgust. "But how Rosalind ever came to be associated with such is wholly beyond me."

Uncertain if her words were falling on good or stony ground, the Countess nevertheless saw no harm in donating her personal assessment of the situation.

"So, Gideon, I have decided that this person is, of a surety, an undesirable *parti* who must, without hesitation, be overthrown. A *mésalliance* at this stage could ruin her chances completely."

"Quite," murmured the Duke, here. "I presume, by your enthusiastic tone, Aunt, you have already formulated a plan of campaign?"

"Yes, Nephew!" She eagerly seized the bait he offered, ere she embarked with gusto on the speech she had rehearsed that very morn. "It is that we arrange for some eligible beau to sweep her off her feet and divert her affections away from this person. Naturally, he must be someone capable of such, who understands the gentle sex and has unlimited experience—in addition to being strikingly handsome, rich, of consequence—er—titled, of course, and gifted with personality and intelligence. Hm-m . . . a sense of humour, whereas not essential, all the same, would not go amiss—and he must be someone we know, Gideon, in order to confide in him, lest he too become emotionally involved. How . . . ev . . . er . . ." she pondered on second thoughts, "It wouldn't matter if he did, as long as he was free to marry—and fulfilled the requirements."

She beamed proudly across at her nephew who reclined at his ease, a sceptical smile playing round his lips.

"And where, may I make s' bold, do you expect to find this Adonis, Casanova and Prince Charming, all rolled into one?"

"That, Nephew, is the most famous part about it!" cried his aunt, hugging herself. "I've already found him!"

The Duke eyed her with grave suspicion. "And he approves?"

The Countess looked a trifle disconcerted.. "We-ll, not

exactly. You see, I thought it proper, first of all, to consult you."

"I see," he acknowledged, regarding the scrolled ceiling. "Am I acquainted with the gentleman?"

"Oh, yes, Gideon—quite well."

"Not my good friend the Viscount?"

"Of course not! He's already moonstruck over Isabella, as you very well know. Apart from which, though he may be eligible in other ways, he is hardly what one would term a scintillating wit."

"I assure you, Aunt," smiled his Grace in defence of his friend, "contrary to outward impressions, his lordship can be quite diverting at times—er—sufficiently stimulated beforehand, you appreciate?"—significantly raising the brandy-glass.

"Which I do not question, Nephew!" retorted the Countess, indignantly. "But I cannot see how a drunken viscount—even one as diverting as his lordship in such condition—could be relied upon to sweep a young girl off her feet, particularly one as lovelorn as your ward."

"Lovelorn, Aunt? Surely you exaggerate?"

"I think not, Gideon. I agree the situation is not yet hopeless, but unless we take immediate action, all will be quite lost!"

"Well—what of Don Juan? All he has to do is weave his magic spell and the day will be saved."

"But, Nephew," she pointed out, dubiously, "—we have yet to ask him, and he may not readily agree."

"I should be vastly surprised if he did. Look at it from his position—what precisely does he get in return for his services, apart from the exhilarating stimulus to his manhood at saving beauteous damsel from tragic fate?"

The Countess gave a despairing shrug of her well-upholstered shoulders, gazing forlornly across at him.

"What else is there to offer when he already has everything?"

"Except a wife—which he probably wants like a ball in the brain!" completed the Duke, relinquishing the glass to begin the inevitable search for his snuff-box. "Correct me should I happen to be mistaken, Aunt," he resumed, running the errant article to earth in one of his pockets, "but do you expect the gentleman to expose himself to such deadly peril, purely as a favour to your good-self?"

"As a favour to you, Gideon!" she expostulated. "Naturally, I'd be loth to see the child ruin her life, but, after all, she is your responsibility."

"I see—and I suppose you would have me approach him with your little scheme, and attempt to influence his decision in your—er—our favour?"

His aunt coloured slightly. "I-In a manner of speaking. . . ."

"Being a particular friend of mine, o' course," added his Grace, inhaling a pinch of snuff with due deliberation.

"We-ll, you could put it that way—"

"A very close friend, in fact. . . ."

The Countess was now strangely disquieted, not at all liking the way her nephew was eyeing her.

"H-However, Gideon," she stammered, hurriedly, "though the plan may not appeal to him at first, he should at least consider the merits of it before leaping to any hasty conclusions—"

"Indeed, so close," he went on, ignoring her, "that we are one and the same—are we not, Aunt?"

"I-I don't know what you mean, Nephew. . . . I—"

"Are we not, Aunt?" he emphasized.

"But, Gideon . . ." She broke off, realising the futility

in protesting any further, then relented with a nod—at which the Duke closed his snuff-box with a snap and, rising peremptorily to his feet, bid her a 'very good-day', declaring he had recalled an urgent matter demanding his immediate attention, as he made for the door—but his aunt forestalled him.

"Gideon—I realise it has probably come as a shock to you, but please pause a moment to weigh the advantages."

"Somehow, all I can see of a sudden are disadvantages," he responded, striving to gain access to the door against which his aunt's stout back was firmly placed.

"But it's as much for your sake as anyone else's! Please, Nephew," she pressed him, pleading. "Don't jump to any impetuous decisions you may later regret. After all, it wouldn't be difficult for a man like you—you've already driven half the female population in London to distraction!"

"Pure conjecture."

"It's the undeniable truth, and you know it!"

"Flattery, Aunt, is something I neither heed nor indulge in. I suggest you try firing from another angle—er—tears perhaps, they're a good persuader—but not today, there's a good woman. I doubt if I'd be much moved in my present humour."

"Oh, you're incorrigible, Gideon! And so obstinate! How does one get through to you?"

"Er—whilst on the subject of getting through things, mayhap you'd allow me through the door?" he requested, making another vain bid to bypass her.

"Why so anxious to leave, Nephew?" she quizzed him, taking his advice concerning her method of attack. "Have your feet suddenly turned cold? Ha! Ne'er did I think to see the Daring Delvray turn such a craven and flee panic-stricken from a mere child!"

This new strategy of his aunt's met with a modicum of success, taking the Duke momentarily aback.

" 'Pon honour, Aunt!" he exclaimed in astonishment. "What new circumvention is this?"

"Tell me, I pray you," she continued, inspired by his thunderstruck visage, "what it is you fear. Were your ward one of the female vultures of Society I could well understand your reluctance—but you know as well as I that she's as meek as any lamb, and totally inexperienced where rak—I mean—er—gentlemen like yourself are concerned. How, then, could you possibly become involved? Surely you of all men, Gideon, so impervious to Cupid's arrow, cannot truly believe you risk losing your heart to this innocent?"

For one brief moment the Countess's flame of triumph waxed strong—until it suddenly petered out when her nephew lapsed into a fit of laughter, to her extreme annoyance.

"Aunt Gertrude," he gasped anon, kissing her affectionately on the cheek. "You're wonderful! I admit 'twas an excellent try—quite ingenious, in fact—and a vast improvement on your last attempt, if I may say so. Methinks you overdid the cowardly bit a trifle, but nevertheless, I must salute you."

"Gideon!" she screamed, piqued, making a final effort to impress upon him the gravity of the situation. "Really! I vow you treat the whole affair far too flippantly. Don't you care what becomes of the child?"

"On the contrary," he replied, deathly sober in a flash. "No one is more conscious of the seriousness of the situation than I, there being a deal more at stake than even you, Aunt, could possibly be aware. Were you fully acquainted with the facts, I doubt greatly if you would consider me such an admirable candidate for your little charade. However, you have my word that I shall devote careful thought to your suggestion, and give you my answer at the ball. Does that meet with your approval?"

The Countess submitted with a sigh "I must own it is more than I expected, knowing how stubborn you can be. Still, I wouldn't wish it otherwise—you're so like your father." She smiled wistfully up at him, adding: "It's just that—well, I have become rather fond of the girl—and she and Isabella are as devoted as sisters—"

"Dash it, Aunt! Spare my tears and let us view the ballroom."

But at this point his aunt happened to glance down and a look of abhorrence transfigured her countenance.

"Gideon!" she shrilled, aghast. "What on earth have you done to your beautiful coat?"

"Ah—something else I inherit from my father, I'm afraid," he replied, ushering her through the door, "—carelessness."

8

Following the Court presentation, time seemed to gather momentum as the ball drew nigh, everyone in a flurry of excitement—infecting even Rosalind and temporarily dulling the ache in her heart which was becoming unbearable, yet which she stubbornly refused to acknowledge.

This excitement had reached boiling point when the appointed hour arrived for her and Isabella to commence their prolonged toilettes for the ball. Having been squeezed unmercifully into stays and laced fit to burst, they were being smothered in countless petticoats when the Countess descended in their midst to ensure they did not over-paint their faces. Be that as it may, her prime reason for intervening just then was to present Rosalind with a silver inlaid ebony casket which had been delivered by liveried messenger—from the Duke. Inside, on a cushion of rich black velvet, lay a priceless tiara, intricately designed with exquisitely matched pearls entwined with silver leaves—at which Rosalind gasped in awe.

But the Countess did not allow her to stand long bewitched, as the first guests were due to arrive within the hour.

"Oh, Aunt Gertrude . . ." breathed Isabella ardently, gazing at her reflection, her dainty figure adorned in a dreamy confection of delicate pink lace, the voluminous skirt caught up here and there with tiny white rosebuds, which also trimmed the sleeves and bodice. "Surely Lord Sevington will offer for me tonight?"

"Not until Gideon gives him leave, Isabella," replied her aunt, attending to Rosalind. "And you know his views on the matter."

"Huh! Gideon will never let me wed!" pouted her ladyship.

"That's not true, Isabella!" contradicted the Countess, firmly. "You must realise, my dear"—she broke off to tug Rosalind's petticoats into place—"that marriage is for a lifetime, not until some other beau takes your eye. I believe there were at least a dozen different gentlemen you were prepared to commit yourself to, during your sojourn in Paris only last year."

"But Lord Sevington is different, Aunt. I've never felt so deeply about anyone before," she vowed in earnest.

"If that is so, Isabella, then it will certainly survive until your eighteenth birthday, as Gideon has promised."

With that, the Countess closed the subject to devote her full attention to Rosalind, whose gown was a magnificent creation in white satin brocade, figured with silver motifs, and styled on majestic lines with a modest train for easy movement. White satin shoes with silver buckles were placed on her feet and a pearl necklace clasped round her throat, as hands plied to and fro bestowing a patch on her right cheek and another, invitingly, on her left shoulder. Next the Countess added the crowning touch by placing the tiara on her head, evoking gasps of admiration all round until the Countess bade everyone make haste.

"Shouldn't Rosalind's hair be fashionably powdered, Aunt?" queried Isabella, on afterthought.

"Why paint the lily purple merely because violets happen to be in vogue?" came a lazy voice from the door.

The Countess and Isabella wheeled round—Rosalind not daring to move lest she fall apart—to find the Duke lounging in the doorway, surveying the little scene through a silver eye-glass set with sapphires, his tall frame superbly clad in cream satin embroidered with gold thread, whilst the customary snowy lace frothed at wrists and chin, and his raven hair lay confined at the nape of his neck by a gold ribbon.

"Gideon!" cried his aunt in protest. "You, of all people, should know better than to intrude at such a time."

"On the contrary, dear Aunt," he corrected her, nonchalantly sauntering into the room to scrutinise his ward at closer range. "You forget, 'tis highly *à la mode* for ladies to entertain gentlemen during their toilettes. I have it on excellent authority that the ablutions of the Pompadour are immensely popular, though a positively frightful squeeze. Faith—one barely has room to raise one's—er—eye-glass, I understand!"

"Gideon!" screamed the Countess, louder than before. "Really! In front of these innocent lambs, too. Whatever that vulgar woman chooses to do is not of the slightest interest."

"I simply repeat what I've overheard on the Society vine."

"Fudge," mumbled his sister. "I wager he's scrubbed her back."

Luckily, this went unnoticed by the Countess who was addressing the maids: "Quickly, girls! Gloves, fan and lilies, that's right!"

Rosalind was then given permission to view herself, and apprehensively turned to see staring back at her the most breathtaking vision she had ever seen. She stood spellbound, unable to make a sound, until tears coursed down her cheeks—evoking a further shriek from the Countess who rushed forward with a handkerchief to dab anxiously at her protégée's face.

"Lud, child! No! No! You mustn't cry at this stage, 'twill ruin the effect completely!"—and grabbing the haresfoot, sought to repair the damage, after which she promenaded Rosalind up and down, made her sit, stand, turn about, and curtsy several times.

During this performance, Isabella acquired permission to go downstairs where Lord Sevington was awaiting her pleasure.

"My task is now complete, child," the Countess then addressed Rosalind, "and his Grace will take charge." Kissing her on both cheeks, she went on: "I wish you every success, but I know of a surety, that by midnight you will hold Society in the palm of your hand."

Rosalind thanked her warmly for all her help, then approached the Duke and sank into a profound curtsy at his feet, eyes lowered.

"Your Grace," she ventured, demurely. "My only hope is that I shall not disappoint you in any way."

The Duke swept her a magnificent bow. "Rest assured, child—your astounding beauty will surely knock the Polite World completely off its axis." And kissing the tips of her trembling fingers, raised her up to lead her from the room.

A full hour after the first arrivals, Rosalind was still honouring the distinguished guests as his Grace presented her, with indefatigable aplomb, to each. She could vaguely recollect him escorting her down the wide curved staircase as if in a dream—where everything seemed to float—and into the great ballroom, a veritable fairyland, with huge gilt-framed mirrors reflecting the brilliance of the chandeliers, casting their radiance round the hall to shimmer iridescently on the silks, satins and brocades of every hue, and incite the myriad jewels to blaze forth their priceless beauty. By now, she was accustomed to the thud of the major-domo's staff which drummed out each new arrival before his sing-song announcement, when she would extend her hand, cursty, smile—her legs already ached terribly, and she had not even begun to dance.

Again came the monotonous thud! thud!—"Sir Francis Romaine, and Lord Peregrine Pringle!" droned the major-domo.

The two swaggered into the hall with an arrogant air—Sir Francis outshining his friend (and everyone else) in ostentation, as he minced forward then poised affectedly —not so much to view the gathering, as for the gathering to view him. This presented no difficulty for he was over six foot tall and fifteen stone in weight—yet despite this handicap, managed to manöeuvre himself quite nimbly. Lest anyone present should be almost blind, he had adorned himself in a flame-coloured brocade, with diamonds twinkling and sparkling in every conceivable place —even amongst his lavishly powdered locks. His nose— by far his best feature—was straight and well formed, but sadly discredited by the remainder of his visage, for his eyes—apart from their deficiency in size—were too close-set, and his lips—of the thick slavering variety—were drawn back in a fixed grin, revealing teeth a trifle decayed in spite of sundry remedies.

Revulsion mounted in Rosalind at his grotesque figure, flaunting a laced scented handkerchief in one hand, and a fan in the other—favouring the latest of whims.

" 'Pon my soul," observed the Duke, rather loudly. " 'Twould seem St. Nicholas has called early this year," at which Rosalind had difficulty in maintaining her dignity.

Sir Francis bestowed a pretentious smile on the Duke, choosing to ignore the remark which he was bound to have overheard.

"Ah, m' dear Delvray!" he gushed forth, in his ludicrous falsetto, with a bow. "Still evading the nuptial noose, eh?"

"I detect no scar upon your own neck, Romaine," parried his host.

"*Touché*!" cried the other, dabbing non-existent tears from his eyes, during which painstaking action he beheld Rosalind.

It must have been one of the few occasions in his life that he found himself bereft of words—but the failing was momentary as he petitioned the Duke in feigned languishing manner, to present him to 'the veritable vision' by his side. The Duke returned a look of contempt, but Sir Francis was oblivious to what he thought as his beady eyes glittered over Rosalind, unable to believe what they saw —like a jackdaw eyeing a hoard of silver.

"Fie on ye, Pringle!" he admonished his friend. "Move along and give others more worthy a chance!"—and before the Duke could make the introduction he seized Rosalind's hand, which he proceeded to devour whilst waxing poetic, eloquently comparing her eyes with the stars—her lips with burgundy wine—her cheeks with June roses—and pronouncing her overall beauty too heavenly for mortal man to look upon—yet lustfully gazing his fill all the same, so close that she could feel his obnoxious breath upon her cheek.

"Damme—steady on, Romaine!" intersected the Duke, viewing the other askance. "If y'r hunger's so deuced rampant why not adjourn to the refreshment room? No doubt you'll find something to appease even your fiend— er—unusual appetite."

Sir Francis resisted the impulse to make a requital, as he was causing an obstruction, and so passed on with a final ogle at Rosalind, performing a bow which almost dislocated his shoulder.

All went well following this uncomfortable episode, Rosalind commencing the ball—partnered by the Italian Prince Alessandro, and in no time at all she was the consummate envy of every female present—particularly the not-so-young misses, unable to secure a partner, who sat with their tight-lipped mammas round the ballroom on plush settees, the tongues of the latter working in keen competition with the elbows of the fiddlers, in the musicians' gallery above. This threw the Countess into transports as she flitted round the room chatting with the guests, and doing all she could to boost the reputation of her protégée.

However, if Rosalind's reputation required boosting amongst the females, it certainly needed no such assistance amongst the males, with whom she was popular on sight. So much so, that the Duke, on abandoning the cards some two hours later, was mildly surprised to find her attended by no less than eight admirers—of whom she seemed totally unaware—which served to inflame their ardour the more.

As his Grace stood indolently contemplating the diverting scene, his aunt bore eagerly down upon him.

"Isn't it wonderful, Nephew?" she burst forth, excitedly. "She's on the tip of everyone's tongue!"

"Quite," he concurred.

"Just look at her—sitting there like a queen amongst her courtiers, and . . . yes, I do believe that's the Earl of Childon's son, Cecil, handing her the cordial—and that's

Vincent Cowan holding her lilies! His father is Viscount Hindle, you know?"

"Yes, Aunt—I know," he responded, lethargically.

"Oh, Gideon! Just think if she were to become Countess of Childon!" She glanced sheepishly up at him. "Or better still, Duchess of Delvray?"

The Duke glanced enquiringly down at her. "I recollect no mention of marriage in your proposition," he blandly observed, idly tapping his toe in time to the stately gavotte being danced.

"Maybe not—but can you deny the possibility?"

"No, I can't," he confessed—his aunt exulting rather prematurely—"because no possibility exists, and never will."

The Countess's face fell downcast. "Then you refuse?"

"Don't you consider eight gentlemen of rank and fortune—not to mention the hundreds more likely to be queuing at the door tomorrow morning—sufficient distraction without my assistance?"

"But they aren't distracting her at all, Gideon!" she exclaimed. "She's distracting them, I grant you—but look at her! She's utterly impervious to every single one!"

"In that case, what makes you so sure I shall succeed where so many have failed?" he casually enquired, focusing his eye-glass on the buxom Miss Selina Rayne drifting by in the dance.

"Don't gammon me, Nephew! You can outdo your whole sex with irresistible charm when you feel inclined."

"Mayhap I don't feel inclined."

"My plan doesn't appeal to you, then?"

"I haven't said so, Aunt. . . . On the contrary," he opined, amusedly playing his eye-glass up and down Rosalind's shapely form, "I find it a stimulating challenge.

. . . However, before you run amock with delight, Aunt, please bear in mind that I dance to no one's tune but my own. I guarantee to cure Miss Tremayne of her emotional disorder, but I do it in my way—without any well-intended interference whatsoever. Are we agreed?"

"Absolutely, Gideon—you always were my favourite nephew!"—and with that she whisked away, leaving the Duke to linger awhile, ruminating his decision whilst pensively regarding the subject of his meditation as she honoured the Earl of Alnstone with her hand for the minuet.

At the end of the dance, Rosalind found herself in company with Rowland and Fiona—soon to be joined by Isabella.

"What a frightful bore the Marchioness of Selcombe is," stated Fiona, confidently to Rosalind. "I thought I should never escape. I simply enquired how her son and heir did, and I vow she detained me a full hour talking of nothing else!"

"Phew! What a crush!" exclaimed Isabella, seating herself beside Rosalind. "Aunt Gertrude will be in raptures."

"It is certainly going well," approved Rosalind, as Rowland—feeling a little *de trop*—took himself off to procure refreshment, shortly after which (to Isabella's joy) they were joined by Lord Sevington, who found to his dismay, the only seat available was alongside Fiona Chalmers who, as can be appreciated, had one or two curious questions to put to him, discreetly out of hearing.

"It is extremely good of his Grace to go to such trouble and expense on Rosalind's behalf, Lord Sevington, is it not?"

"Hum—er—yes," affirmed his lordship, not caring for

the road the conversation was to take.

"Particularly so when they are in no wise related?"

The Viscount nervously smiled his acquiescence.

"I understand from the Countess," she pursued, doggedly, "that Rosalind is the daughter of an intimate friend of the Duke?"

"S-So I believe."

She flashed him a meaningful look which he seemed unable to meet.

"Was it not an odd turn of fate, then? I mean, how he came to . . . to . . ."

"Er—odd indeed," concurred the Viscount again, cogitating how best to satisfy the lady's inquisitive mind and save his face. "Hum—being in ignorance of her birth, and lacking means of support, she had chosen that certain way in which to—hum—mitigate her straitened circumstances, you—er—understand, and chanced to fall in with the other—hum—rogue."

Rowland, having returned during the course of this stammered revelation, here voiced his sentiments—noticeably unsteady.

"B' Gad! G-Good thing . . . G-Gideon's coach, what? May not have b-been s' f-for-fortun—er—lucky, eh?"

This was unanimously supported by the two, and thus encouraged, and somewhat inebriated, he went on: "M-Might have d-one a . . . vashtly dif-diff'rent dansh to-to the m-minuet ere now. . . ."

His listeners gasped, visibly shocked, as it was obvious he referred to the Tyburn Jig.

"Rowland!" ejaculated his wife, glancing swiftly in Rosalind's direction, lest she had overheard. "You are intoxicated!"

"I believe I am, m' dear," he confessed, striving to focus

his dilating eyes on her. "Deushed shorry if I caushed off-offence. . . . Fiona . . . Shev . . . ington—never c-could take m-more . . . than three . . . glashes without com . . . ing . . . unshtuck."

"Three glasses! More like thirty-three, the condition you're in!" flung back Fiona with vexation.

The Divertimento by Haydn had ended and everyone was taking the floor for a contredanse, for which Rosalind and Isabella were already committed, and so the Viscount hastily retreated to the cardroom to escape the domestic wrangle between Rowland and his wife.

Each dance she danced Rosalind's heart grew heavier, because her partner—though rich and handsome—was not he for whom she yearned. And this dance was no exception. Even when it ended, her eyes still searched the throng for possible sight of him—alas!—not only to be disappointed in this, but to spy the King of Fops clearly headed her way. At first, she tried to conceal herself amongst the crowd, but on he came, his eyes adhering avidly to her shapeliness as she weaved in and out, hoping to shake him off. In desperation, she seized the only means of escape—through the French windows into the gardens.

Here, she readily inhaled the balmy night air, a cool breeze playing round her flushed face as she luxuriated in the peaceful atmosphere after the stifling overcrowded ballroom—at last able to give licence to her thoughts.

She wandered aimlessly along the rambling paths in between the matured flowerbeds, gazing up at the heavens aglitter with stars, her heart seared with the now familiar longing for the man she had grown to love so profoundly. Her heart pounded anew, as she thrilled again to the memory of the magical moment when she had floated with him down the stairs on a cloud of intoxication, and entered the dazzling ballroom—how the touch of his hand had fired her blood, and how she had battled madly against the feeling of weakness and desire which had threatened to overwhelm her, lest she faint outright at his feet. Did he suspect? Was he aware that her bemused condition was due to his nearness, and not the excitement of the occasion? Never before had she been so close to him, and the feeling he evoked in her was frightening!

But if she was prepared to accept the fact that she was hopelessly, passionately in love, what was perhaps not quite so easy to accept was that the man she loved was not only a callous rake who cared for no one but himself —but who openly despised her, and was simply manipulating her like a puppeteer—using her as bait to lure his quarry into his trap—the one woman to mean anything to him—her mother.

Was he now dead to that tender feeling—or had he merely erected a barrier of cynical indifference, to protect himself from further humiliation and pain? Rosalind did not doubt that beneath the frigid exterior there lay dormant a deep turbulent love which, if roused, would brook no resistance, but sweep aside all in its path. If only he would lower his guard long enough for her to coax it to life! What did she care if she were engulfed in its ungovernable fury?

She paused by the ornamental pond, watching the goldfish weaving patterns in her reflection—when an alien sound broke in on her reverie, the tap-tapping of high heels, as if the wearer were anxious to approach unheard, and spinning around, found herself confronted by the offensive leering visage of Sir Francis, his thick lips drooling with lascivious intent.

"Egad! Found ye at last, Moon Goddess!" he squawked, like a drunken parrot. "Basking in the light o' y'r domain up yonder."

"La! Sir Francis," she cried, forcing a light vein as she nimbly evaded him. "I vow you quite startled me."

"Rot me! Keep still, will ye? Nearly had me in the demned fishpond! Y're as elusive as a confounded butterfly!"

But Rosalind continued to flit round the pond in an effort to humour him, always managing with a swish of silks to elude his grasp—until she had the misfortune to slip on a wet patch, and he seized her in his lust-craved arms.

"Got you, me tantalising temptress!" he panted, his hot stale breath scorching her neck. "Now 'll show you what I do with baggages who play cat and mouse with me!"

But before he had a chance, she sank her teeth into his hand and with a yelp of pain he sprang back to land—red heels uppermost—amongst the startled fish! Rosalind did not linger to hearken to his spluttered curses, but whisked up her skirts and sped indoors, leaving him to the excellent offices of the footmen who at once ran to his aid. His coach was hailed forthwith and he was borne away, convulsed with anger, brandishing an outraged fist at the four dumbfounded footmen.

9

Rosalind experienced little enthusiasm for the divers invitations which arrived in profusion during that week, her mind being wholly centred upon the man to whom she had eternally relinquished her heart. Indeed, her engagement diary was so full that it was—to her despair—almost six weeks before she was free to attend the play at the Theatre Royal with the Duke, Isabella and the Viscount—and a further two months ere she could join the Duke's party for a trip to Vauxhall Gardens.

Upon the evening in question, the party of eight—including the Earl of Alnstone (already besotted with her)—travelled to the Gardens in the popular manner along the Thames, and upon arrival, had not sauntered long amongst the fine display of illuminated cascades, dancing bears, monkeys, jugglers and magicians, when the Duke met a group of intimates whereon he suggested the rest of the party continue to the amphitheatre, where he would see them anon. And so, the remainder went on to view the many booths housing the diversions, to a background of seraphic music—though perhaps her ladyship and Lord Sevington were too rapt in each other to heed music, seraphic or no, but mindful even so, to stay close to the rest of the party, out of danger of the mob. Alas, Rosalind did not take such stringent precautions!

All may have been well had she not been magnetically drawn to a fire-eater from the mystic East, who had mesmerised so many people with his act that the crowd at this point was particularly dense. So much so, that she had not stood long entranced when she felt herself jostled, then pushed and shoved before the crowd grew violent and finally ran out of control. As she tried to fight her way out she tripped on her gown and would certainly have fallen to be trampled underfoot had not a pair of muscular arms grabbed her from behind and lifted her bodily out of the mêlée.

On recovering from her stupefaction at being miraculously delivered, she turned to thank her gallant rescuer—to suffer yet another shock, as she stared up at her archenemy, Sir Francis Romaine, across whose revolting features was carved—seduction!

Unleashing a cackle of exultation, he bore her off through the shrubbery, clutching her to him in hungry possessiveness, equally deaf to her protests to let her go as he was impervious to her fists drumming on his broad chest. His eyes were glazed with lecherous desire as he carried her some distance away, panting breathlessly, unable to comprehend his good fortune, while searching for a convenient spot to commit his dastardly deed.

After her first futile attempts to free herself Rosalind decided to conserve her energy for the fray which was to come. She could hear the murmur of the crowd growing fainter in the distance, to be eventually obliterated by the giggles and groans of doubtful goings-on in the undergrowth around her.

At length, he must have found a place to his satisfaction, for he suddenly dropped her down on the grass like a sack of vegetables, then stood astride her, arms akimbo, and unleashed a spine-chilling laugh of sadistic triumph—at which Rosalind may have burst into tears, had not she been in such a towering rage.

"Well, my snooty beauty—what have you to say?" he gloated, gazing smugly down on her helplessness. "Gave you a surprise, eh?"

"Which is nothing to what you'll get if you don't release me immediately!" she spat, furiously—which merely induced another guffaw of harsh laughter, sending shivers down her spine.

"Don't rely on your Dissipated Delvray to come to your rescue," he chortled. "He'll be too busy with some wench behind yonder bush! How many times has he had willingly what I'm about to take by force? Doesn't fool me by calling you his ward! Ward—mistress—*fille de joie*, if you prefer it in French—they all mean the same!"

"You licentious pig!" she yelled at him, forgetting her drawing-room manners as she tried to rise, but he roughly pushed her down again. "He's never touched me!"

"I wouldn't lay a wager on't!" he snarled, looming over her. "Anyway, tonight you are mine, my delectable damsel, and there's nothing he or you can do about it! I've plotted this ever since you—with your smug conceit—pushed me into that damnable pond, for which I now claim overdue reckoning!"

And with a savage lunge he flung himself on top of her writhing form, knocking the wind out of her, as he tore madly at her gown, his thick wet lips descending unremittently on her face, shoulders, breasts, while his hairy spatulate hands mauled her tender white flesh like a barbarian.

At last, able to inhale some air into her lungs, Rosalind screamed an ear-splitting scream with all her might, but still his scornful laughter rang out in defiance.

"Scream away, my pretty," he crowed. "They're all too

busy playing the same game round here to heed a scream or two."

Exhausted, she sank back to recoup her strength for the final onslaught—which he misinterpreted as surrender, and emitting a whoop of joy, raised his great bulk to lunge to his ultimate conquest. To be temporarily relieved of his unbearable weight was all Rosalind needed, and plunging her feet into his chest with all the force she could muster, managed to knock him off-balance.

In a flash, she was up and off across the grass, her disordered skirts fluttering as she ran wild-eyed and panic-stricken back along the way they had come, thankful for the head start his state of undress had given her. She dodged in and out of bushes, tripping over bodies lying sprawled at intervals, running on, sobbing hysterically, but forever urging herself on towards the friendly murmur of the crowd—now growing louder. How her breath and legs kept her going she had not time nor wits to ponder, but with his irate cries far behind she pressed on, driving herself until she thought her lungs would burst.

Even when she reached the main avenues she did not slow down, but still ran blindly on, causing no little stir as she ploughed through the throng in a state of shock-mania —until she was suddenly brought up short by her arm, seized in a rigid grasp which would not be thrown off. Reaching the end of her endurance, she flew at her adversary like a ferocious tigress protecting her young—to be ruthlessly shaken, but to the bissful sound of a very familiar voice.

"By the saints! I'll certainly think twice before assaulting you on a dark night without my abigail!"

These words fell on her ears like sweet music, and Rosalind ceased her raving to raise her anguished eyes in incredulity to the equally astonished face of her guardian. Never, if he lived to eternity, would the Duke forget that tortured look before it changed to recognition and unspeakable joy as she threw herself with a heart-rending cry into his bewildered arms.

"In heaven's name, child—what's happened?" he exclaimed, blenching at her ravaged state.

Finding her too overcome to speak, the Duke guided her away to a secluded seat where, in the comfort of his embrace, she gave licence to her grief, clinging to him in desperate need, while he remained silent, his face hardset.

Eventually her tears subsided and she sat up to dry her eyes on his proffered handkerchief, self-consciously drawing the remnants of bodice across her exposed bosom.

"Is Romaine responsible for this?" he demanded suddenly, his hand clenching involuntarily on his sword.

She nodded dumbly, eyes downcast.

"That swine's tried my patience long enough!" he rasped —more to himself, rising to his feet.

Not daring to believe what he intended, Rosalind grabbed his arm as he made to leave, leaping afoot also.

"No, your Grace!" she cried, horrified.

"Stand aside!" he snapped—but she rashly persisted.

"P-Please, your Grace—your life is much too valuable to waste on such as he . . . an-and you would never find him—he's bound to be miles away by now."

Appreciating the truth of this, he halted, staring down at her, the glint in his eye so murderous she could not meet it.

"How far did he get?" he challenged.

She struggled to reply, but the words stuck in her throat.

"Look! I realise it must pain you damnably to speak of

it, but I've got to know! Did he—"

"No!" she cried out, at last. "He didn't get that far!"

"Thank God for that!" he sighed, sinking back on to the seat in evident relief.

"You need lose no sleep over it, your Grace!" she added on a bitter note. "My honour is firmly intact and I'm still an eligible candidate for the marriage mart, if that's all that bothers you!"

"Now just a minute, young lady! Granted, it may be all that bothers me, but I have suspicions of a third party who, methinks, might show an interest."

"Th-third party? I-I don't know what you mean."

He eyed her shrewdly. "I think you do," he observed, calmly. "Do you deny being a trifle off-colour of late?"

She reddened profusely and averted her face into the shadows, understanding the point he was making.

"Yes—er—I-I mean—no! I-I mean, I agree, I have not been quite myself recently, but surely it isn't surprising with all the excitement—the ball an-and ev-every . . . thing."

He did not seem convinced. "Nothing more serious?" he queried, suavely. "No organic disorder—like heart trouble, for example?"

Rosalind nervously screwed the damp handkerchief into a ball, her prolonged silence proclaiming her guilt.

"I see—well, now that we've diagnosed the complaint, all we have to do is prescribe a cure," he elucidated with an offhand gesture. "However, permit me to state at the outset, whereas I appreciate the untimely moment for raising such delicate topics, I'm afraid urgency compels me to speak out. You detect my meaning?"

She nodded hesitantly, devoured with misgiving—and

noting her discomposure, his manner became a little more sympathetic.

"Rest easy, child, there is no cause for alarm. I merely seek answers to one or two questions. This man—he is eligible?"

Again she nodded.

"Indeed?" Her guardian seemed surprised. "He has wealth? Title? Position?"

Rosalind acknowledged all three, generating an element of suspicion in his mind, but he made no comment.

"Are you much stricken by him?" he probed, furtively.

She bit her lip, gave an indeterminate shrug, then stammered: "I-I think so."

"You think so! Surely you know whether 'tis serious or not?"

"I-If you mean serious enough for marriage—then yes, it is."

The Duke studied her downcast face, debating within himself. "I did not intend mentioning it just yet," he resumed at length, "but I have already been approached by three aspirants to your hand—"

"S-So soon?" she gasped in horror.

"Well, you did create quite a stir amongst Society's gay blades—and you aren't far off twenty, y' know"—adding apologetically: "I'd have softened the blow, but you did force my hand."

Rosalind raised her eyes to the bejewelled heavens— oblivious to the magnificent fireworks display in progress, the rockets streaking across the sky to explode in a million coloured lights, evoking shrieks of delight from the crowd on the embankment—a delight her despairing heart forbade her to share.

"If I may say so, Rosalind," pursued his Grace, gently,

"you do not appear to cherish much hope—he lacks interest, perchance?"

She nodded with a sigh.

"Ah!" was all he said, but with a wealth of meaning.

'If only he wouldn't look at me that way,' she pleaded, inwardly. 'He isn't making my position any easier.'

He leaned forward to place a hand on hers, of a sudden —unaware that he was straining her resistance to breaking point.

"I may not inspire confidence, my dear, but you evidently need someone to confide in—perhaps you would grant me the honour?"

'Stop! Stop! If he will only stop!' the small voice cried out. 'He is so near'—that inviting shoulder where not a moment ago—oh, ineffable joy!—her head had actually lain . . . so near, in fact, that ever and anon the breeze wafted strands of his long black hair across her cheek, weakening her, until she was unable to control her words and any moment liable to fling herself into his arms, blurting out everything.

"Has this man any knowledge of your feelings toward him?" he asked on impulse—and meeting a negative response, went on, a hint of enthusiasm in his voice: "Well, then—why admit defeat? Many men are reluctant to proclaim their affection for fear of rejection. Do you think 'twould help if I were to intercede on your behalf? I mean, if he is one of Society's outstanding catches we are bound to be acquainted. I assure you," his voice fell to a whisper, "I can be the very soul of discretion."

Rosalind smiled despite herself, at this encouraging effort on his part, bethinking it strange how a man so uncommonly astute could discuss himself thus without even realising it.

"Thank you for the kind offer, your Grace—"

"Faith, child! I'm not trying to be kind," he protested, candidly. " 'Tis as much in my own interest as yours to see you well established. With whom, of course, doesn't perturb me overmuch, but there is your father to be considered. However, if 'tis possible to combine all, 'twill be to everyone's satisfaction—wil't not?" He cast her a sidelong questioning glance. "What manner of man is he, anyway? Is he partial to female company?"

"H-He doesn't seem to be," she admitted, ruefully.

"So, he is impervious to your coquetry and looks." He smiled cryptically to himself. "We're evidently two of a kind, he and I—mayhap he also has excellent cause to shun your sex?"

"Mayhap he has!" Rosalind retorted. "But we aren't all determined to lure every man to his doom!"

"No matter—it just requires contamination from one member to ruin a man for life."

"Surely he could be cured," she challenged him, "by the right woman—a woman who loved him deeply and sincerely?"

She now managed to meet his gaze, but oddly enough, he seemed unable to meet hers and his eyes wandered away to feign an interest in the cherry trees arbouring the seat.

"I fancy you aren't going to give up easily," he remarked, anon.

"No, your Grace," she avowed. "I mean to find his Achilles' heel!"

He threw her a curious glance. "You are sure he—er—has one?"

"Hasn't everyone?" she parried slyly, "—even your noble self?"

The Duke did not confirm one way or the other, but lounged back, indolently surveying the globular lamps suspended overhead.

"You haven't got long, y' know—the Season ends in a few weeks. Doubt if you'll stand much chance of engaging the enemy after that. And what of your suitors? Can't expect them to languish for ever."

"But I need a little time. . . ."

"You shall have a period of three months to make your conquest," he declared, decisively. "If, by the end of that time, the gentleman insists on remaining a bachelor, then you must admit defeat and select someone more appreciative of your charms—agreed?"

"I-I agree," she pledged, failing to realise the impossibility of the task she was setting herself.

He rose, leaving her to ruminate his ultimatum, and plucked a handful of blossoms from an overhanging branch, then beckoning her to stand before him proceeded to arrange them deftly in the neck of her torn bodice, as if it were his regular custom.

"There's no need to blush, child—you are by no means the first female to benefit from my artistic genius."

She had no alternative but to stare up into his studious face as he effectively arranged the flowers.

"A-Am I so very like her, your Grace?" she ventured, cautiously.

"Like whom?" he murmured, engrossed in his work.

"M-My mother."

"There! That should serve," he observed, eyeing his work critically, before answering. "Your likeness is beyond belief—but pray don't feel disillusioned. Your mother was incredibly beautiful . . . the most beautiful woman I have ever known—and the fact that you resemble her so closely should be sufficient compliment in itself."

"But wasn't she . . . b-bad?"

He gave licence to a twisted smile. "Rest content—you resemble her only in looks," he opined, running his eye over her with an air of satisfaction—until it arrived at her hair. "Hm, your hair is rather bedraggled. . . ."

Rosalind made to oblige, but as she swept it back he hurriedly stopped her, cursing at sight of the ugly bruises standing out vividly against the whiteness of her neck and shoulders.

"Er—p'raps 'twould be wiser to leave it the way it is. Should my aunt's vigilant eye alight on those scars she is sure to ask some extremely awkward questions." Adding humorously: "Of course, you could say you'd been attacked by a bear."

"I think I should have preferred it," laughed Rosalind.

"Who's been attacked by a bear?" suddenly piped up a third voice, evoking a groan from the Duke who recognised his sister's cry.

"Gideon! Where on earth have you been? It's quite late and I . . ." She broke off as her round brown eyes—growing even rounder—caught sight of Rosalind's disarray, whilst Lord Sevington loomed up behind. "Good gracious, Rosalind!" ejaculated her ladyship, on closer inspection. "Have you really been mauled by a bear?"

Rosalind ashamedly shook her head, wishing the Duke would come to her aid with some plausible explanation, but at present he seemed otherwise preoccupied with his own appearance.

"Well, you certainly look as though you had—doesn't she, my lord?" But the only response forthcoming from the Viscount was a discreet cough and a mumbled incoherency. "Unless . . ."—her eyes swivelled suspiciously in her brother's direction. "Gideon! What have you been doing to Rosalind?"

"I beg your pardon?" he queried, dragging his attention away from the lace beneath his chin.

"Really! I am thoroughly disgusted that a man of your years should stoop so low as to . . . to . . ."

"I am thirty-six, 'Bella, not ninety-six!" he cut in, sarcastically, whilst his lordship's elegantly powdered head pivoted from one to the other, hoping to discover the truth. "Miss Tremayne had a slight mishap with a bush."

"A bush!" echoed her ladyship. "But her gown is torn to shreds!"

"Oh, Lady Isabella! It's not that bad," expostulated the Viscount.

"Er—'twas a holly bush," casually amended the Duke, unabashed.

"I don't believe a word of it! You are lying to save your own skin—but you don't deceive me! Just wait until Aunt Gertrude—"

" 'Bella!" burst in her brother, cutting her dead. "When we get back to Cavendish Square, should you as much as hint that I am responsible for Miss Tremayne's tattered condition—I shall have a few things to say about your own rather dubious conduct."

Whilst her ladyship sought to regain her voice, the Viscount sought to vindicate his conscience.

"I-I naturally assumed that Lord Alnstone and Jeremy were escorting Miss Tremayne, as they all seemed to disappear at the same time. And as Lord Halleston was unfortunately obliged to leave rather hurriedly with Lady Halleston, who became indisposed—it left only your—hum —sister . . . and . . . my—hum—self."

"Quite," accorded the Duke, glancing significantly from

one to the other. "Not one moment of which heaven-sent opportunity was wasted, I'll warrant."

An agonising silence ensued whilst her ladyship hid her confusion by proffering Rosalind her domino, and his lordship gazed skywards at the moon, as if suddenly noticing it.

"Gadzooks! 'Twould seem I stand at odds here," resumed his Grace, with irony. "Whilst all and sundry have been cavorting about in the bushes yonder, I—reputed to bear a soul blacker than a witch's cat—have wandered alone, innocent of thought and deed, rapt in appreciation of Mother Nature's beauteous gifts."

"Y-Your Grace!" gasped Rosalind.

"Egad, Gideon—coming it rather strong!" protested his friend.

"Gideon!" exclaimed Isabella, making herself heard above the rest. "If that was meant to be a sample of your singular wit, it was in shocking bad taste, and not at all amusing!"

Her brother threw her a mocking look. "Guilty conscience, 'Bella? I swear, 'twas not my intention to cause offence—I was merely generalising—and to prove my goodwill, I shall entertain you all to an abundant supper, for which you must surely have acquired an appetite. . . . Come! I have bespoken a table."

10

Rosalind's Season ended in a climax of excitement, finding herself fêted and fawned upon wherever she went, also—dearer to her heart—frequently in the company of her guardian, but suffered a faint disappointment that although he made her gasp in awe at the wonders of London he unveiled before her eyes, bubble with laughter at his lively wit, and went out of his way to gratify her every whim—not once did he impose upon their ward-guardian relationship, or venture a single overture to which the most punctilious Society dowager could possibly object.

However, something which did help to compensate, was the abrupt disappearance from the London scene of Sir Francis Romaine. Following his monstrous behaviour at Vauxhall, perhaps this was understandable—but the Fop King was not the type of person to show a clean pair of heels when scandal reared its ugly head. On the other hand, he may have realised rather late in the day that the Duke of Delvray was not to be trifled with after all. This she could well understand, if his Grace was the master-swordsman that rumour had it—not that she found this easy to credit, for her guardian did not seem capable of dragging a sword from its scabbard, let alone defending his honour with one!

And so, the Season drew to a close—leaving Rosalind within no further sight of her objective. But she did not despair, bethinking her chances of seducing the Duke more advantageous in the intimate seclusion of Claremont Park.

Thus, she meditated her future, and as she did so upon this late June afternoon, it chanced that the other Tremayne—her father, Sir Roger, likewise sat meditating her future, in his study at Tremayne Grange.

It was all too wonderful—that no less than eight eligible gentlemen should have requested the Duke's permission to address his daughter—not to mention five of them bearing titles and immense fortunes—and one actually being a Marquess!

He was, perhaps, just a trifle crestfallen that his daughter had not so far shown a distinct partiality for any particular one, but he had not the slightest doubt that in time one would stand out from the rest, and she would have no difficulty then in selecting he destined to be her husband. Love, of course, would come later, as often was the case. Naturally, she herself would prefer to wed a man she loved beforehand as all young maidens dreamed of, but one had to be practical in these matters. Love could certainly complicate one's life—as he had learnt to his bitter cost.

So, Sir Roger sat at his writing desk on this warm summer's day, poring over the Society column of *The London Gazette*, which gave a substantial report of Rosalind's coming out. This, he vowed with fatherly pride, he would treasure in memory of this significant occasion, hoping one day to have the joy and privilege of reading it to his grandchildren.

But yet again was the Tremayne happiness fated, as an alien sound was suddenly borne in to his ears—of voices raised in angry dispute which were barely audible at first, but gradually grew louder and louder, Sir Roger's brow creasing in perplexity upon recognising one of them as undisputably a woman's. It was unusual in itself that anyone should be visiting him at all, but that his caller should be female was even more so—as the voice was certainly not that of his daughter, who had been first to spring to mind. No, this was a shrill coarse voice which shattered the balmy afternoon, as the conflict raged immediately outside the study door, between the female in question and Simon, Sir Roger's faithful old retainer.

Sir Roger rose, to investigate the commotion, when the door burst open to admit the intruder, flinging a vulgar oath over her shoulder at the menial who was as hotfoot on her tail as his creaking joints could manage. Still in doubt regarding his unexpected visitor, Sir Roger was about to enquire into the disturbance when she turned to confront him. His eyes started from his head in abject horror, emitting a gasp, then a groan, before he collapsed into the chair behind him, burying his anguished face in his hands to blot out the execrable sight of the one he loathed more than any other being on earth . . . his wife, Eugenia!

There she stood, the disruption of so many lives, the stunning beauty with her glorious golden hair reduced to a dull straw thatch which stuck out at peculiar angles from beneath a scrap of tattered black veiling, the solitary remains of a once fashionable bonnet. Any trace of her former loveliness was obliterated by cheap harsh cosmetics which diminished rather than enhanced her looks. Her eyes, while being the same deep blue as her daughter's, were albeit, cold and calculating, with obvious signs of loose living, and her former soft bow-shaped lips now hard-set in permanent aggression. Though somewhat small in stature, she nevertheless had a way of making her presence felt.

Old Simon coughed discreetly from where he still stood,

rooted in the doorway. "I-I regret, Sir Roger, there was nought I could—"

Eugenia kicked the door shut in his face. "Shut up, you old fool!" she yelled in a voice strident enough to make the very furniture wince, before turning back to her husband, seething with rage. "Some grand welcome for the prodigal wife, I must say, when I'm refused admission to my own home!" She tapped her foot in annoyance as her husband slowly raised his drawn face to meet her look. "Well?" she went on. "Have you nothing to say to your long-absent spouse?"

"Yes!" he snarled at last, his thin rounded shoulders heaving convulsively. "Get out! Go, woman—whilst you are yet able!"

This evoked a burst of raucous laughter from her. "Go? Go where? You are my husband, remember, and this is where I belong. I've come home to roost, Roger, whether you like it or not."

To substantiate this statement, she flopped down into the self-same chair his Grace had occupied, her legs straddled in ungainly manner, while Sir Roger struggled violently to maintain his self-control.

"You are not my wife!" he spat at her. "I'm astounded that even you have the shameless arrogance to show your face here again!"

"Let me remind you, sir, that I am still Lady Tremayne, and I belong here as much as you! You took me for better or worse twenty-two years ago and as far as I recall we are still man and wife!"

"You couldn't get any worse! You aren't worthy of the name 'wife'." He was about to add 'or mother' when he curbed his tongue in time, not wishing to divulge anything at this stage.

"Whilst on the subject, sir, you aren't exactly my idea of a perfect husband either! 'With all my wordly goods I thee endow', you vowed, and I've had to fight tooth and nail for every penny—not to mention cutting yourself off from civilisation out here, living like a recluse and expecting me to do the same." She flashed a glance of burning resentment. "I was young and beautiful—I wanted to enjoy myself—show myself off to Society, which was what I married you for—but you had other ideas! You wanted me to tie myself down with swarms of screeching brats and cut myself off from the gay life and all my friends."

"Well!" Sir Roger bellowed back at her. "You got your gay life and friends, so why have you come back to plague me?"

"Because after spending three months in the Bastille I discovered I no longer had any friends!"—and as she ranted on with her nauseating account of the foul conditions inside the gruesome fortress, Sir Roger took the opportunity to review his desperate plight and formulate some plan of counter-attack.

His first reaction of anger and defeat now gave way to calm reason, as he began to analyse the situation, deciding that this unprecedented arrival of his wife was not going to complicate matters. There was only one person to be considered—Rosalind, and her future was not going to be threatened in any way. That Eugenia constituted a threat was a major understatement! If her evil mind ever discovered recent events she would do all in her diabolical power to turn it to her own advantage, and ruin her daughter completely with her insane jealousy—indubitably so when she scented his Grace of Delvray behind it. This, Sir Roger was going to avoid no matter what the cost. Having welcomed his daughter back from the grave, he was certainly not going to stand by and see her future jeopardised by this vile she-devil he had endowed her with for a mother.

There was only one way this could be permanently guaranteed, he thought, with a warm glow of satisfaction, and that was to fulfil his promise made in the Duke's presence . . . she must be disposed of, without delay! He had not the slightest compunction about carrying out his threat as he had nothing to lose, and everything to gain for Rosalind's sake—indeed, would sacrifice his very life to preserve her future well-being. But he did not really credit that the need for this supreme sacrifice would arise as it was fairly safe to assume that, having newly arrived from across the Channel, no one would know of his wife's whereabouts—furthermore, the situation of his estate was a decided advantage, out in this desolate wilderness where an entire army could be massacred without occasioning remark. The only two persons he would need to confide in were Joseph the stablehand, and Simon his manservant, both of whom could be trusted implicitly—Simon in particular, who had served Sir Roger for over thirty years and despised Lady Tremayne almost as much as his master.

Vowing to carry out his foul deed that very night, Sir Roger then simulated an interest in his wife, in order to deceive her into believing all was forgiven, and thereby gain her confidence. He even devoted time and energy to attending her every wish—ordering Simon to prepare her old boudoir which had been locked up for years, in his eagerness to prove he was still the old besotted fool she had always believed him.

Upon informing her that dinner would be served in an hour, she declared she could not wait that long, and took herself off to the kitchens to see what was in the larder.

Whilst she was gone, Sir Roger locked away the precious newspaper inside his desk, carefully pocketing the key. But barely had he done so, when the door swung back on its hinges, and his wife stood in the doorway once again— this time, brandishing a chicken leg in one hand and a bottle of claret in the other. She was clearly labouring under severe emotional strain for her sagging bosom heaved tumultuously, and her hollow eyes smouldered with suspicious indignation.

"The high-flying gentleman you entertained here some months ago," she snapped at him, her hunger taking second place to this crucial issue. "Who was he?"

Sir Roger prevaricated, rattling his brain for a plausible answer. "I-I don't know whom you m-mean—wh-what gentleman?"

"Don't lie to me, you hypocrite!" she screeched at him, hurling the chicken leg across the room to skim the top of his wig and land with a thud in the far corner. "Apparently the cook is much more talkative than that old idiot, Simon. She said you were honoured by a most distinguished visitor—a dark handsome member of the Quality, who measured the height of the door, and was dressed fit to kill! Unfortunately, she couldn't remember his name, but I can! It was Delvray, wasn't it? . . . Well?"

"Yes! Yes!" admitted her husband hastily, as he saw the wine-bottle about to follow the chicken leg.

"And you weren't going to tell me, were you?—Were you?"

"Y-Yes, of course I was—the m-moment wasn't yet opportune."

"For that kind of information, any moment is opportune! You must think me an imbecile!" she snarled. "What did he want?"

"W-Want?" stammered Sir Roger.

"Tell me what he came for, you clodpole!" she yelled with impatience. "Was it me? Was he looking for me?"

Her husband emitted a harsh laugh, unable to resist it. "Oh, yes—he was looking for you all right!"

His wife glanced at him suspiciously, misinterpreting his odd humour. "You never were any good at hiding your jealousy. He was the only man I ever loved! I would have been Duchess of Delvray now had it not been for you!" She paced restlessly round the room like a caged animal, wringing the bottle in her hands. "Every single night for two solid years I wished you dead, after that tragedy. I even invoked the aid of the Devil himself, but still you lived! Why? Why?"

"Believe me," retaliated Sir Roger, livid with anger, "I likewise frequently asked the same question of the Almighty about you—why you should be permitted to walk His good earth leaving a never-ending stream of misery and anguish in your wake!"

"Which proves how much notice even the Almighty takes of your supplications!" she mocked him, gulping down the claret directly from the bottle and wiping her hand across her mouth in disgusting fashion. Sir Roger averted his head, sick with loathing, which she must have noticed, to comment: "I haven't been too particular about my choice of company recently."

Drops of wine trickled down her black gown—rather the worse for wear and bespattered with a variety of other stains, which her husband had mistook for the pattern of the material—as she sprawled in the chair opposite him.

"Well?" she prompted, irritably. "What did he want?"

"That, I am not at liberty to say," returned Sir Roger, deliberately baiting her.

"Why?" she rounded on him.

"You'll find out soon enough."

Her excitement mounted visibly. "H-He's coming back?"

"He didn't say so."

"Have done with your riddles, you old goat!" she screamed, at the end of her tether. "Does he want to see me or not?"

"I believe he does—"

"Because he still loves me . . . after all these years . . ." she rhapsodied, a far-away look in her eye.

"Don't be ridiculous!" cried her husband, out to spike her guns.

"Of course he must love me, you jealous fiend!" she shrieked in fury. "Why else would he come all this way?"

"A little matter of vengeance," responded Sir Roger with a sneer.

"Vengeance? Why should he suddenly want vengeance?"

"Apparently he has never abandoned his quest for it," he informed her with deepest satisfaction. "I think you will find anon, that his Grace is a completely different proposition to your other erstwhile lovers. He doesn't give up so easily."

If this was designed to discourage her it unfortunately had the adverse effect.

"Doesn't give up loving me so easily, you mean! He must love me madly to be thus enraged after so long," she flattered herself, gazing enthralled at the ceiling. "But then, Gideon always was a passionate boy."

Her husband choked on a swift intake of breath. "My dear Eugenia!" he exclaimed, with a laugh. "If you are by any wild hallucination expecting the boy you once knew, let me correct you here and now! He is a wholly different being—even you wouldn't recognise him! He is hard, ruthless and very much in command of himself."

"Until he sees me, my dear Roger, then his hard heart will melt and he'll succumb to my charms just like old times—my slave for life . . . he often said so . . . even knelt at my feet and kissed them once. . . ." She smirked to herself at the recollection.

"You are so puffed up with your own conceit that you just can't see it, can you?" he thundered, determined to convince her of the Duke's true feelings once and for all, lest she take it into her head to set out for Claremont Park there and then. "Don't you realise, woman, that he's no longer the young broken-hearted boy you left behind, but a confident fully-matured man?"

She still refused to be intimidated. "Is he married?"

"No—but I—"

"There now!" she taunted him with a triumphant sneer. "Isn't that sufficient proof that he still bears a torch for me? Would not he otherwise be wallowing in wedded bliss?"

"Or you could have killed any love he had, stone dead!"

"What! Gideon?" She cackled a hollow laugh which made Sir Roger wince. 'All she needs is a broomstick,' he thought, as she went on: "He had enough love in him to keep a harem happy for a lifetime! Ha! You'll need to concoct a more convincing lie than that, dearest husband, if you expect me to believe you." She pushed her haggard face close to his, to hiss contemptuously: "It really incenses you, doesn't it, that a man like Delvray should love me so?"

"Gad, woman—he positively abhors you!"

This statement cost him a resounding slap across his left cheek.

"You'll pay for that, harlot!" growled Sir Roger, tenderly caressing his inflamed cheek—but she merely gave vent to her coarse laughter then had further resource to the bottle, thudding it down on to the desk.

"I've been called a lot worse than that in my time, Roger. You can't shock me."

"I'm sure you have! It doesn't surprise me in the least —just look at yourself." He indicated the mirror hanging close at hand. "Tell me, dear wife, do you honestly believe that the present sight of you would make Delvray weak with desire?"

Eugenia could not help blenching as she came suddenly face to face with herself, but soon rallied round, her spirits undaunted.

"That can soon be remedied," she spat, and stormed upstairs.

However, her husband could not suppress a gasp of admiration at her transformation when she emerged from her room half an hour later to join him for dinner, dressed in a gown of lavender silk, retrieved from her old clothes chest. Her hair she had vigorously brushed, compelling it to shine with its former lustre, and though it defied her wishes, it nevertheless hung down on to her white shoulders quite attractively, while her face had been thoroughly scrubbed and lightly powdered, in an attempt to conceal the ravages of time. Finally, she had added a faint touch of colour to her lips and cheeks, and whilst her eyes retained their hard sunken look and her mouth its severity, the overall effect was astounding.

Yet, despite this miraculous change in appearance, Sir Roger found to his cost during the meal, she was still the same base, vulgar shrew beneath the facade. Not only did she insult him by listing her conquests one by one, but actually went on to befoul his ear with vivid accounts of their sordid methods of misconduct. Sir Roger strove to disregard his wife's abominable revelations, and for a while managed to concentrate his thoughts on his nocturnal plan to rid himself of her once and for all.

The evening ended as it had begun, with a blazing row, and Eugenia sweeping off to her room in a vile rage. Left to his own devices, Sir Roger expended the time debating the precise manner in which to perpetrate his crime— grimacing as he carefully weighed each process according to its expediency.

Strangling was the first method—which he immediately rejected due to his deficiency in physical strength. Eugenia would be bound to struggle violently and the odds were she would overpower him, and his opportunity—if not his life—lost for ever. Shooting was too noisy—he did not wish to alarm the entire household. And the very thought of stabbing made his blood run cold! The only other convenient way was to poison her, but to his knowledge he did not have anything suitable in the house.

Far would it be from anyone's deliberate intention to name Sir Roger coward, but ultimately a plan formulated in his mind whereby he could evade his distasteful ordeal, yet benefit equally well. In fact, the more he pondered his new idea the more it pleased him. He realised he was under an obligation to his Grace, but as his brain had been consumed with thoughts of attaining his own selfish vengeance it had been entirely overlooked. He owed the Duke a profound debt, which he could never hope to repay—except by granting his one request . . . to be given the chance to take his long-awaited revenge on Eugenia.

It had been the only condition his Grace had stipulated —surely the least he himself could do was acquiesce? It suddenly appealed enormously to him! If Eugenia refused to accept his word regarding the Duke's change of heart, then perhaps she would believe the Duke himself when confronted with him.

In a fever of excitement, he began planning what must be done. He would enlist the services of Joseph, who would ride post-haste to London and give his Grace the news. If the Duke had not already left for Claremont Park, then he would be at Tremayne Grange by afternoon —if Joseph left before dawn. Meanwhile, he would lock his wife in her room to give her no means of escape.

The clock on the mantelpiece chimed midnight.

'Perhaps,' he decided with a yawn, 'I will wait another hour, to ensure she will be asleep'—but before long, he himself was reclining in the arms of Morpheus.

Sir Roger awoke with a start! What had caused him to waken so suddenly he could not say, but shrugging off the feeling, he glanced at the clock—astounded to see the hands pointing to a quarter after four. Dawn was beginning to break!

Quickly rallying himself, he crept stealthily out of the study to rouse Joseph and give him his instructions. When he returned, he sat awhile until certain that Joseph was well en route to London, then went upstairs to bed— locking the door of his wife's room on the way and retaining the key.

He reawakened at almost ten o'clock, emitting a groan as he recalled the previous day's events, realising that they were not just the remains of a ghastly dream after all, and rising, he washed and dressed as usual, then crept quietly downstairs—pausing outside his wife's room to listen, but all was deathly quiet. She would no doubt sleep out the morning, he told himself—after her tiring journey, and being overcome with fatigue.

Consuming a light breakfast, he then settled down to await the screams and shrieks of abuse which would assuredly burst from his wife when she discovered that she was imprisoned in her own bedchamber—and the arrival of her illustrious executioner. Sir Roger rubbed his hands together with glee as he visualised the entertainment about to take place. What exactly the Duke would do, he had no idea—maybe hang her up by her thumbs and whip her— drag her behind his horse six times round the estate—or brand her with red-hot irons like they did in France? Perhaps he would strangle her after all . . . surely he would have strength enough even if his long porcelain-like fingers did seem as though they might break with the strain.

He picked up a book, read three sentences and threw it down again, then began to pace about the study in the first stages of restlessness. It was getting rather late, yet there was no response from Eugenia. In seven minutes it would be mid-day! He continued in ever-increasing concern until the hands of the clock revolved to twenty past two —then twenty past three—still there was no sound issuing from his wife, and furthermore the Duke had not yet come. Had ought gone amiss? No less than eight times during the past hour had he summoned Simon to enquire news of Joseph, but the reply was always the same— Joseph had not returned.

By four o'clock Sir Roger was exceedingly distraught, and he was still pacing the floor—when all at once his eye was arrested by something white protruding from the lid of his desk which was, in fact, nothing more than a scrap of paper. To anyone less methodical it may have seemed innocuous enough, but tidiness was an obsession with him and it struck him as extremely odd that he should have left his desk in this disorderly fashion, so he at once crossed the room the better to investigate.

Grasping the lid, he tried to raise it—expecting it to remain firm, but to his astonishment and dismay, it opened quite easily—and what met his gaze made him blanch with horror. Not only had the lock on his desk been forced open, but that of a small strong-box placed therein which had contained fifty guineas. It was disturbing in itself that the money had gone, but what alarmed Sir Roger even more was that a handy-sized pistol which he kept by him for protection had also disappeared. Panic seized him as he recalled to mind the newspaper but to his immense relief he spied it still emerging from between the books where he had originally placed it.

At this point a knock sounded upon the study door, heralding a much travel-stained Joseph, in a state of collapse from his exhausting journey, and who was welcomed with eager arms by his master. His news, however, was disappointing to say the least. Apparently the Duke had already left for his estate when Joseph arrived in St. James's Square, the housekeeper informing him that his Grace's equipage had departed that very morning, only one hour earlier. Joseph vowed he had tried to catch up with the Duke, but to no avail.

Sir Roger swallowed his despondency and, patting Joseph on the shoulder, discharged him from his duties for the remainder of the day.

The next problem was Eugenia, and as he mounted the stairs to her boudoir in feverish haste, yet did he refuse to give credence to the doubts in his mind striving for recognition. But as he turned the key in the lock his misgivings surged to the fore, warning him that he would find the room empty—and wrenching open the door, discovered sure enough that it was.

Not only was the room completely deserted, but it appeared that the bed had not been slept in as the coverlets were undisturbed, except for the impression of her body where she had lain on top awhile. Sir Roger fell weakly against the doorpost, wiping a trembling hand across his damp forehead in an effort to ward off the faintness which threatened. His brain spun in confusion as he battled to assemble his bewildered thoughts, beginning to suspect what his subconscious mind had already established as fact. It was not until he stumbled down the stairs in a stupor of disbelief that his head suddenly cleared and full import was borne upon him of his wife's malicious intent. Obviously she was already on her way to Claremont Park to establish once and for all if the Duke still loved her, and when she discovered the answer, the pistol would ensure that he would never love anyone else.

However, if Sir Roger deemed this the absolute limit of his tribulations he was due for an even greater shock when he hurried back to his desk to double-check if anything else was missing, for during his search he chanced to snatch up the folded newspaper and his blood congealed in his veins—to find the entire page concerning Rosalind's presentation torn savagely out, and the remains cunningly refolded to appear still intact.

Prostrate with grief, he collapsed into the nearest chair, his worst fears realised. Eugenia knew everything and was on her way to exterminate her supposed opposition to the Duke's heart . . . her own daughter, Rosalind.

11

Sir Roger sank into the depths of despair, relinquishing all hope of ever saving his beloved daughter. His brain was now too old and feeble to compete with his wife's evil genius. If he had only summoned enough courage to carry out his dastardly deed the night before and put an end to her wickedness once and for all, his daughter's life would not now be in this deadly peril.

But surely the Almighty had not given him Rosalind back just to let this infernal witch cut her down, he asked himself, the thought infusing hope into his shattered frame, and with it the energy he desperately needed. Perhaps all was not yet lost? True, Eugenia had taken his only horse —apart from that which Joseph had brought back from London exhausted, but the tired animal would get him to the nearest village where he could procure a fresh mount. And it was highly unlikely that she would traverse the entire distance to Claremont Park on horse, which would give him some advantage. She would probably abandon the horse at the first inn in favour of a more comfortable form of travel. But he would surprise her! He would show her he was not the weakling she thought him! He must be gone—at once!

Ringing his hand-bell peremptorily for Simon, he ordered the worn-out steed to be resaddled, adamantly refusing to hearken to the protests of him and Joseph alike, when they discovered his intention. He would not even permit Joseph to accompany him when he offered to ride pillion to Wisborough Green then hire another horse, but pointed out to allay their anxiety that he stood every chance of overtaking the Duke on the road, who would be slowed down considerably by his extensive retinue—trusting Eugenia did not do so beforehand.

As Sir Roger was setting out, his wife was already well on her way, having departed at the unearthly hour of four that morning in the hope of reaching the Duke's estate the following day—but exceedingly hampered by her skirts and the muddy roads, she was soon forced to postpone her vendetta. At the first coaching inn, she eagerly exchanged the horse for the public stage—as her husband had foreseen, unaccustomed as she was to riding, and not being equipped for it.

Words could not describe her fury when she had stumbled upon the information about her daughter during the early hours, whilst ransacking her husband's study for anything of value—even as he slept soundly in his chair close by—unaware of how near he was to receiving a ball through his head for deceiving her! But she had already conceived a more fiendish plan in her mind.

She smirked in satisfaction as she jogged along on her journey, bethinking she could not have his Grace of Delvray in a better position if she had personally contrived it. She fondled the pistol in the tapestry-bag concealed beneath her cloak, but was convinced it would not be necessary, for when his eyes drank in her beauty he would crumble like newly baked cake and again fall a slave to her charms.

There seemed little doubt that the King of the Underworld was indeed in league with Eugenia, in the way a certain fashionable beau offered to accommodate her in his chaise and guarantee to get her to her destination ere she could blink her bewitching blue eyes, for which—he made obvious—he expected to receive her favours in exchange, at the first inn they chanced upon. Eugenia readily agreed to the proposition—prepared to trade her very soul if need be, unable to say if she were more over-joyed at making such great headway, or flattered at attracting the attentions of such a fine elegant gentleman. Evidently she had not aged as much as her husband was wont to think.

In fact, the only discomfort she was obliged to suffer was compassing the distance from the lodge gates of the Duke's estate to the main door, afoot, which was no mean feat, as from the gates the great house was barely discernible on the horizon. Nevertheless, she accomplished it, goaded on by the prospect of finally realising her ambition, whilst the ache in her legs was alleviated by a perpetual round of maledictions. Keeping furtively in the bushes lining the drive (not wishing to be seen and thus forewarn the Duke of her approach) she at length reached the door and gave a vindictive bang at it with the brass gryphon's head knocker—as if it were responsible for her long tiring trudge—then waited, mentally reviewing the conglomeration of lies she had concocted en route.

Anon, a footman answered her summons, of whom she requested an audience with his Grace—only to be informed that the Duke had not yet returned from London. Unfortunately, her ladyship was also out, visiting on the estate, which left no one but Miss Rosalind at home.

In feverish curiosity Eugenia begged to be admitted, and once over the threshold, dismissed the flunkey, expressing a desire to surprise the young mistress as she was already on acquaintance with her. Dubiously, the footman bowed, and after indicating the door of the main drawing-room where Rosalind was, withdrew. Pausing until the servant was out of sight, Eugenia then threw back the veil screening her face, to survey herself in the huge mirror on her immediate right and pat a curl or two into place, after which she shook out the folds in her satin gown of warm cherry, which—though not in the height of fashion —had the miraculous effect of subduing the hardness of her face. Her hair, however, was arranged in the latest mode, and having washed and brushed it thoroughly the previous night, it now glowed with something of its former glory. She herself was immensely pleased with her reflection, and replacing the veil over her face, approached the drawing-room door upon which she tapped lightly, then entered.

Rosalind sat by the window browsing through a current issue of the *Ladies' Magazine*, with the brilliance of her golden hair reflected by the sun. Glancing up in surprise, she rose to welcome the unexpected visitor—perhaps as well for her that the visitor was heavily veiled, concealing the consummate envy which swept across Eugenia's face when her eyes alighted on her daughter. She reeled suddenly, for it was like coming face to face with herself as she had looked twenty years ago. Incensed, she battled inwardly to regain her self-control, determined not to ruin everything at this point.

However, upon closer scrutiny, Eugenia abandoned her fears, for it became obvious that her daughter was not experienced in the ways of the world and the desires of men—like she herself, which would surely throw her in the Duke's favour. If Delvray was as mature as her husband would have her believe, then he would doubtlessly prefer to bed a full-blooded woman, rather than this slip of a girl, still wet behind the ears!

Following the exchange of greeting, Eugenia's burning jealousy compelled her to avert her eyes from this dazzling vision in lemon brocade, which seemed to illuminate her in the sunlight with a radiance like some immortal being.

With supreme effort, Lady Tremayne began the conversation.

"You do not know me, my dear," she ventured, sweetly, resuming after a negative reply: "I am a very old friend of the Duke, which gives me unfair advantage, for he has told me all about you."

"R-Really?" faltered Rosalind, puzzling whom the lady might be, as she proffered her a chair.

"And when I read this colourful description of your recent coming out," went on her mother, presenting the news-sheet purloined from her husband's desk, "I felt an overwhelming urge to call and see your astounding beauty for myself." To admit this cost Eugenia dear, but she managed to quell her bitterness.

Rosalind blushed as she took the paper, and after a cursory glance, placed it on a table beside her. She then offered some refreshments which her mother civilly declined—indignation bubbling up in her at her daughter's condescension, as if she already considered herself mistress of Claremont Park!

"Tell me, child," she queried, simulating a composure she did not feel. "Have you resided here long?"

"Almost a year," responded Rosalind.

'Long enough for him to be tiring of her prosy innocence and fancying a change,' thought her mother.

"Won't you give me your name so that I may tell his Grace who has called?"

This threw Eugenia into some confusion. "Oh—er—I-I am . . . Lady Lewis," replied she, hastily assuming the name of the gentleman she had passed the night with.

"Lady Lewis?" repeated her daughter, thoughtfully. "The name is not familiar—but I'm sure his Grace will be desolate at not seeing you."

"Are you expecting Gid—I mean, his Grace to return very soon?"

"Within the next few hours, according to the message received."

"Good!" approved Eugenia. "Then I trust it will not inconvenience you if I linger awhile? Having travelled a distance, I should be loth to leave without seeing him."

Rosalind smiled her appreciation and there ensued a tense silence, broken at length by Eugenia, anxious to establish the relationship between her daughter and erstwhile lover.

"Do you live here alone with his Grace, my dear?"

"Certainly not, Lady Lewis!" exclaimed Rosalind, shocked at the lady even thinking such an indelicate thing. "His sister, the Lady Isabella, also lives here."

"Sister?" echoed Eugenia, knocked off guard—for the Duke had never referred to his baby sister, who had been a tender sixteen months at the time of their association— but rapidly comprehended her error. "Oh, y-yes, of course . . . the l-ladyship the footman mentioned, his sister— how silly of me, I had quite forgotten. I-It's been so long, you see."

Rosalind nodded politely but remained unsure. That Lady Lewis should be unaware of Lady Isabella's existence struck her as uncomfortably strange. Why should his Grace furnish the lady with a glowing account of she herself, yet fail to mention his own sister?

"Then you and he are not—er—" Eugenia broke off at the horrified look on her daughter's face.

"I-I beg your pardon?" stammered Rosalind, hardly daring to credit what was now passing through her guest's mind, as she grew more uneasy in the company of this extraordinary woman who was becoming a little too personal for comfort. If Isabella would only return!

"Please don't misunderstand me, my dear—I am on very intimate terms with his Grace and naturally take a friendly interest in your welfare. You may speak quite openly to me—as you would your-er-mother."

'What unusual talk for a casual caller,' thought Rosalind, still listening for sound of Isabella.

"Would you be offended if I were to ask a rather personal question—a question your mother might ask?" pursued Eugenia—her daughter wondering what sort of questions she had been asking all along. "May I ask how you feel toward the Duke?"—Rosalind gasped, but her mother hurried on, determined to plumb the depths of the relationship. "Are you in love with him? Tell me!"

Close friend of the Duke or not, thought Rosalind, this woman had no right to question her so, but she could not risk openly offending her. She floundered helplessly, casting about for a way of escape, when—to her unspeakable joy—her eye alighted upon the one person she needed more than any other—the Duke, himself.

How long he had stood in the doorway eavesdropping on the conversation, was impossible to say—but probably long enough to take stock of the situation.

Howbeit, if the Duke's presence took Rosalind by surprise, it was nothing compared to the effect it had on the visitor. Starting to her feet, she stood like a stone pillar, clutching the table behind her for support before snatching away the veil to stare, drawn hypnotically to the one man she had ever yearned to possess body and soul, her bosom heaving turbulently beneath her cloak at him thus catching her unawares.

But the Duke looked magnificent! Even Rosalind had never known him look so devastating—dressed head to foot in black, relieved only by the lavish silver embroidery on his coat of stiffened brocade, and the snowy ruffles at throat and wrists—while his black hair rested loosely on his shoulders, framing his handsome face—as inscrutable as always.

Eugenia remained spellbound, unable to tear her eyes from him. She had thought him handsome as a youth, but now, as a full-blooded man, he was positively lethal! Those eyes . . .

Rosalind, trying to fathom why the lady's face should appear familiar, suddenly broke the electrifying silence.

"M-My mother . . ." she whispered in awe, her voice barely audible. "Y-You are my m-mother."

"Yes!" flashed Eugenia contemptuously, not averting her gaze from the Duke. "I am your mother! And now you will see, daughter, how a man reacts to a real woman!"—and tossing away her cloak to reveal her charms—which were daringly exposed—she slowly began advancing towards the Duke.

Although she would be the last person to admit it, Eugenia was in her fortieth year but even so, had lured most of the French nobility to her boudoir—as well as English, and was still capable of doing so when she set her mind to it—as she had proved only last night at the inn. And now, as she traversed the room, her face shone with its former beauty, the hard features melting in a bewitching smile directed at the Duke—whose eyes never deviated from hers.

Rosalind drank in every movement, now well able to

understand how his Grace had fallen hopelessly in love with her. The witchery of her appeal radiated from her with a dynamic force, almost supernatural. Would he weaken at the crucial moment? Had he truly conquered the evil magic of her power over him? She devoutly prayed so, for it was about to be given its supreme test!

Eugenia's voice coaxed him soothingly, in low dulcet tones.

"I have come back to you, Gideon, to beg your forgiveness for all the years of agony I have caused you. Nothing has changed, my beloved—I am still your Eugenia who loves you to distraction! I have suffered too, my dearest—years of unbearable remorse, but I shall make up for all the pain and heartache you have endured. I love you, Gideon, as I have always loved you—there has never been another man who could take your place."

Rosalind was in a fever of torment! Her mother was only feet away from him now! What would he do? Would he resist her? Oh, he must! He must! She could not bear the thought of him seizing her mother to him in an ardent embrace, forgiving and forgetting the sixteen years of his dear life she had ruined—when she herself loved him so profoundly and felt sure she could bring him the happiness he so richly deserved. But if not, what was the frightening alternative? She tried to define his look, but his face was devoid of all expression as Eugenia drew even closer.

"Leave the room, Rosalind!" his voice rang out suddenly, making her jump.

"No!" objected her mother, halting only six feet away. "Let her stay. She may learn from my experience."

This made Rosalind no wiser regarding the Duke's purpose. If he made passionate love to her mother, or murdered her, both would be equally improper for her to witness.

As his ward made no move to obey his command, the Duke closed the door gently behind him, his green eyes still riveted to Eugenia, who had resumed her machinations.

"I didn't ruin everything between us, Gideon—it was my old fool of a husband! But now that I have returned, we can go away, just the two of us, until the old bas—er—until he passes on—or I could have him dispatched at once! Anything! I'll do anything for you! Eventually we could be married, and you could return here with me as your Duchess—"

Rosalind uttered an inarticulate cry, horrified at her mother's callous scheming, which drew a look of scorn from Eugenia.

"It doesn't matter about her! I don't know how she happens to be breathing anyway! Heaven knows, I paid her assassin plenty! But she's no problem—we can soon auction her off! Even if you have had your way with her, my over-zealous love, she can still snare a wealthy husband. You and I know she's not as pure as she looks, but I can show her countless ways to convince a doting spouse otherwise! I vow, I am an absolute master at the art!"

Rosalind clapped her hands over her ears to shut out the sound of her mother's accursed tongue.

But now came the crucial moment as Eugenia finally reached the Duke and began to press her body seductively up against him, gradually sliding her arms up round his neck when he did not object, luxuriating in the feel of his powerful shoulders beneath the silken brocade as her face progressed closer and closer to his—the Duke remaining perfectly still, unnaturally so, offering no resistance to her armorous overture. A glow of triumph swelled inside her —and when she felt his hand begin to creep encouragingly up her back, then his long fingers twining in her hair, she almost whooped aloud with joy at winning him over so easily! . . . Until his lips twisted in a savage snarl and his eyes blazed with a thousand demons as he tightened his grip on her hair—tighter, tighter—dragging her back and back, she too stupefied to make any sound, wondering what he was about—when his other hand shot up to lock round her throat in a brutal stranglehold.

Eugenia emitted a strange gurgle, threshing the air with her arms as he ruthlessly applied pressure, choking the life out of her, his fingers not relaxing for an instant as her face slowly turned from crimson to purple, her eyes bursting from her head.

Rosalind screamed and rushed down the room to tear frantically at the Duke's hands in a desperate attempt to release their vice-like grip on her mother's throat, and glancing up at his face, she blenched at the fiendish smile of satisfaction manifest, as—with hellish delight, he at last attained his long awaited revenge.

Furiously, he ordered her to stand aside, but she ignored him, realising that even his illustrious position would not save him from the law if he murdered the wife of an aristocrat in cold blood—and frenziedly renewed her struggle to separate them, wrenching at the Duke's right arm till he momentarily released his hold to thrust her angrily aside—which opportunity Eugenia seized to drag herself free. Stumbling blindly, she retreated to the opposite end of the room far out of reach, rubbing her inflamed neck whilst her eyes smouldered poisonously at him—Eugenia, the aristocratic lady, now Eugenia, the vicious hell-cat.

Meanwhile, the Duke threw off his madness and sought

to recover his composure at the wine-cabinet, while Rosalind returned to the window-seat, devoured with anguish —about to see her mother in her true colours.

"I see it all now!" spat Eugenia, glancing from one to the other. "She's bewitched you! Turned you against me with her angelic airs and graces—but wait till she's seen a bit of the world and reaches my age, she'll be just as rotten as I am!"

"I'll be damned first," murmured the Duke, downing a large brandy.

"What's happened to you? You loved me once!"

He flinched at the reminder, unable to look at her. "I was but a callow youth who knew no better. I couldn't love you now if my life depended upon it." He replenished his glass, then seated himself on the arm of a chair, glass in hand. "You aren't fit to own a viper for a daughter, let alone that innocent creature!"

"Innocent!" screeched Eugenia. "After living a year 'neath your roof? Personally, I thought you would prefer the more experienced woman—men of your age usually do—instead of abducting schoolroom chits to ravish in your own private brothel!"

Once again did the Duke urge Rosalind to leave, but as before, her mother intervened.

"She will stay! What I have to say concerns her more than anyone!"

Her hand still involuntarily caressed her bruised throat, whilst she stared maliciously at the Duke—always mindful of her distance. But her caution would seem unnecessary, for apparently he was now in no hurry to wreak his vengeance. Rosalind's intervention had been fortunate! On consideration, strangling was too quick and with a quick death he was being merciful, from which he would derive little satisfaction.

"It is this," she went on. "In future, Bacchanalian orgies with my offspring will cost you a handsome penny!"

"Mother!" cried Rosalind, her stomach heaving in revulsion.

"So," smiled his Grace, unruffled. "We arrive at the crux of the matter . . . my wealth! A generous slice of my fortune in exchange for your daughter's reputation—is that it?"

"Exactly!" she snapped, battling to devise a way to lay hands on the pistol which was still in the bag, and lying—of all places—at the Duke's feet. "A slice for the exhilarating entertainment, and a bigger slice to keep my mouth shut!"

To her surprise, the only response this evoked was a groan from her daughter, and she sensed the first pangs of discomfort—though unable to say why. Obviously the Duke was not labouring under the acute disconcertion she had anticipated, as he indolently drew his silver-hilted sword from its scabbard and proceeded to toy with it, provoking her to visible signs of agitation.

"Well?" she prompted irritably. "What have you to say?"

With infuriating precision, he put down the brandy-glass. "You appreciate, you are in no position to dictate terms?"

"Then you dictate the terms," she proposed quickly, foreboding roaming in the pit of her stomach. "Make me an offer—if it's reasonable, I'll take it and leave you and your doxy in peace."

But the Duke showed greater interest in his sword which he upheld to the windows to play the sunbeams, flashing and gleaming up and down the cruel blade.

"A-A few thousand will do," she persevered.

"Alas! Methinks you've had a wasted journey, Lady Lewis," he sneered with disdain. "For you will get not a few pence—but pray do not be disillusioned . . . you will get something."

Eugenia felt trapped—now realising the truth of her husband's words. This was not the languishing youth she had known! Here stood a complete stranger, deadly sinister under the courteous facade which he would discard at any moment to reveal the satanic being beneath. How her fingers itched to get at that pistol!

"Wh-what do you mean?" she stammered in genuine alarm—whatever it was, surely he wouldn't dare?

The Duke rose suddenly. "Enough of this play-acting!" he snarled, testing the balance of his sword. "Providence has allowed you to go unpunished too long for the heinous suffering you have inflicted on mankind—it is time I assumed command!"

Numb with fear at the terrible nightmare she was living, Rosalind, realising the danger in interfering, nevertheless cried out: "Your Grace! What do you intend?"

"First of all, you must catch me!" taunted Eugenia— regaining a modicum of confidence as he began to step away from the bag . . . but towards herself, ever so slowly, like a stealthy black panther stalking its prey. "Surely you cannot hate me so intensely?" she pleaded, endeavouring to keep up the conversation and distract him from her purpose. "Isn't there a grain of that old feeling left?" She took refuge behind a high-backed chair, shivering involuntarily at the menace in his green eyes as he still advanced. "You can't have forgotten how you once loved me, Gideon," she pursued, unaware that her words were goading him beyond reason, "when you held my naked body close to your own . . . caressing me with those beautiful hands . . . before you—"

The Duke lunged at her with the lethal weapon—which she evaded only by a hair's breadth, as it slashed through her gown. He evidently meant business!

"When I finally despatch you to his Satanic Majesty, he will have a permanent record of your past conquests carved on every inch of your flesh!" he hissed through his teeth, having finally cornered her, and coming in for the kill. "I can reel off a dozen names to begin with, but first of all—my own!"

"No!" shrieked Rosalind, defying the Duke, and again assisting her mother by leaping up to throw herself bodily against his sword-arm, risking the full blast of his wrath in a frantic attempt to prevent bloodshed—and as before, Eugenia took her chance and sped down the room to fumble feverishly in the bag.

By the time his Grace—in a towering rage—succeeded in ridding himself of Rosalind's encumbering weight, Eugenia had retrieved her pistol and was aiming it steadily at his noble person. Immediately aware of the danger to Rosalind as well as himself, the Duke furiously ordered her to get out whilst he kept her mother under guard.

"If she takes one step towards that door, this ball goes through your callous heart!" threatened Eugenia, licking her lips in satisfaction at sight of her victory. "As you see, my Lord Duke, I came prepared for all eventualities," she went on smugly. "Roger said you had changed, but even I never expected you to be the hellish swine you are, Delvray. All the same, if I'm going down below, you're coming with me!"

"Then fire and be damned!" thundered the Duke, beginning to suspect she did not intend shooting him at all, as she backed furtively away to embrace Rosalind in her line of fire.

"You and I are both rotten, Gideon," she continued in wheedling tone. "That wilting lily's no good to a man like you! She's only after what she can get, but you're so possessed by her you just can't see it. She already fancies herself your Duchess with her sanctimonious affectation, lording it over me! Me—who would have been Duchess years ago had it not been for my dotard of a husband!"

The Duke side-stepped, blocking her view whilst awaiting a chance to seize the weapon—longing to flash a glance behind at Rosalind, yet not daring to relax his vigil on her mother.

He was about to call out and warn her when Eugenia brought the situation to a rapid climax, and deftly evading him as he drew within reach, yelled wildly: "If I can't be Duchess, neither will she!"—took swift aim, and fired.

There was a deafening report and the ball whizzed across the room with uncanny accuracy towards its target, striking Rosalind just above the left temple—leaving an ugly red gash in its wake. In three strides the Duke was at her side to catch her as she fell, while Eugenia battled frantically with the French windows to gain her freedom as she could already hear the sound of footsteps running to investigate the explosion—when the windows gave way, precipitating her out into the grounds. Picking herself up, she set off fleet of foot across the lawns towards the driveway with the anguished cries of servants echoing in her ears. On she sped without a glance, the palpitating beat of her heart drumming in her head, already applauding herself at thus managing to escape the Duke's wrath, when she spied a rider coming up the drive towards her. This did not alarm her unduly, until the gap between them narrowed sufficiently for her to distinguish the features of —her own husband, Sir Roger.

Abruptly, she cut off to the left, through the trees, hoping by some miracle that he had not seen her—but her red gown stood out vividly against the green background, enabling Sir Roger to spot her at once and steer his tired animal in her direction, coaxing new life into it with a pat on its perspiring neck, as the cries of the approaching servants became recognisable.

"Stop her! Stop her! She's shot Miss Rosalind!" Some were yelling that Rosalind had been killed, but this Sir Roger did not pause to find out as, incensed with a fiendish madness, he goaded his animal across the green after his wife—who was now headed for the woodland bordering the grounds—where she obviously thought she stood a chance of shaking him off. But Sir Roger gave a further spurt to his horse, infusing it with his own super-human energy as he charged along like a demon from the underworld, with one phrase recurring in his head, 'Rosalind is dead! Rosalind is dead!'—beating a tattoo in his fevered brain in rhythm with the hoofbeats. By now he had covered the incline and gained the level stretch where he began to narrow the gap rapidly—there she was, two hundred yards ahead, more staggering than running— now only one hundred—now only fifty. . . .

As he drew closer Eugenia could feel the horse's breath on her back, the beating hooves dinning in her ears, and glancing behind, her eyes protruding from her head in terror, she suddenly tripped on her torn gown and fell headlong—while her husband, his face distorted with indescribable hatred, bore down mercilessly upon her.

Her screams for clemency fell on deaf ears, mingled

with the whinnies of her husband's steed as he reared and plunged it relentlesly down on her, its hooves mutilating her beyond recognition. Even when she lay a still, mangled heap, he kept on and on in his savage grief at what she had done to his daughter.

But suddenly his madness left him, and drawing his horse to a standstill, fell on its neck prostrate with exhaustion, and the crucifying agony of the terrible thing he had done.

12

It was a considerable time and several brandies later, that Sir Roger showed signs of recovering from his state of shock and exhaustion, as he lay prone upon a daybed in the study at Claremont Park, attended by the Duke, who stood by his side with tight lips and clenched hands—the only outward signs of the tension consuming him. Gradually, the colour flowed back into the older man's lips, enabling him to speak.

"R-Rosa . . . lind? Is—is she . . ."

"Alive, thank God!" burst forth the Duke, availing himself of the brandy he held—formerly intended for Sir Roger.

"Th-thank God, indeed!" gasped the other, closing his eyes with overwhelming relief.

"My sister returned a short while ago," went on his Grace. "She is with her now. I have, naturally, already sent for my physician—he should arrive at any moment."

Sir Roger opened his eyes to gaze wretchedly at his host—who paced restlessly about the room—noting the dull stain on his elegant sleeve where Rosalind's head had lain when he had carried her up to her boudoir.

"I could have made away with her two nights ago," Sir Roger burst out, violently, unable to contain it any longer. "And would have done, had I not been such a craven! How I detest myself!"

"Don't reproach yourself, sir," besought the Duke, pausing to comfort his guest. "I am to blame more than anyone for prizing my vengeance and selfish pride above all else—it was unforgivable! I can't think what possessed me—it is not in my nature to become so incensed."

"Eugenia had that power over me, too—the power to goad one beyond endurance. But I've made certain she'll not do so again!"

Here, in disjointed sentences, Sir Roger explained how his wife had met her ghastly death, which the Duke termed an unfortunate accident, and would be reported as such. Sir Roger then went on to relate all that had happened since Eugenia's painful advent at Tremayne Grange, in exchange for which, the Duke gave his version of all that had transpired at Claremont Park—ending with the shooting disaster. Then, declaring himself equal to the ordeal, Sir Roger begged to be taken to see his daughter, in order to reassure himself that she was indeed alive. At first, the Duke tried to dissuade him, but he was so determined that his Grace finally consented—much against his better judgment.

Rosalind had been put to bed by the maids, supervised by her ladyship, who was still much stricken by it all, having rallied bravely round—to her brother's mute admiration, at his urgent request for her to give assistance, and so had tended the wound herself, to the best of her poor ability.

She alone remained in attendance when Sir Roger and her brother entered the room and approached the four-poster bed, to see Rosalind lying unconscious, like an angel from heaven amongst the white, rose-trimmed organza drapes and sheets—though with an unnatural pallor in her cheeks, and breathing barely perceptible.

Suddenly, the deathly hush which had fallen all around was disrupted by her father, who collapsed on his knees by the bed, sobbing over one of her limp hands.

"M-My child . . . my d-dearest . . . child! Y-You must . . . l-live!"

Isabella sank to her knees beside him in consolation, an arm round his thin shoulders.

"I swear, Sir Roger," vowed the Duke, solemnly, "everything humanly possible will be done to ensure that she does."

His Grace turned away, unable to bear the horror of gazing upon the fulfilment of his long-desired vengeance, and retraced his steps to the door, as if anxious to be gone. Sir Roger rose with difficulty to his feet and bent towards his daughter as if about to kiss her, but changed his mind when the door opened to admit a maid who heralded the doctor's arrival.

The medic blustered into the room, clutching his black leather bag as if it contained his very life—bowing to the assembled company and wishing them a good afternoon although it was now evening. After a perfunctory glance at the patient he turned to detain the Duke.

"A shooting accident, I believe, your Grace? Those—er—confounded poachers again, eh?"

He pursed his lips in a soundless whistle as he peered over the top of his spectacles awaiting the Duke's reply. But the Duke merely smiled condescendingly, leaving his physician to interpret this whichever way he felt inclined.

"Hm," went on the doctor. "Had no end of bother m'self! Determined to get the scoundrels one of these days, b' George!"

At length, the physician emerged to inform the Duke and Sir Roger that the patient was an extremely lucky young woman to be alive—something they already knew. Fortunately, the wound was only superficial and would

probably heal in a week or two—but she had lost an
alarming amount of blood and was in an exceedingly weak
state. He could not pinpoint the hour when she would
regain consciousness—possibly well into the night. And
with that, he took his leave, declaring he would call again
on the morrow.

Now that everything possible had been done for Rosalind, Isabella left her in the care of the maids and joined
the gentlemen below for dinner, urging the girls to call her
if necessary.

Anon, the company of three sat down to dine, but—
understandably—no one appeared to be very hungry despite not having eaten for several hours, and no sooner
had the wide variety of succulent dishes been arrayed upon
the table, than the footmen were ordered to remove them
again. Sir Roger was then prevailed upon by his host to
retire to his room for a well-deserved rest, as it was unlikely that his daughter would revive for some time. This
Sir Roger sensibly agreed to do—when the Duke had
promised on oath to rouse him the instant she opened
her eyes.

Brother and sister now remained, seated at opposite
ends of the long table which was adorned with the customary gold and silver plate, candelabra, flowers, and
wine decanters. His Grace lounged back in his chair,
clasping the burgundy in one hand and his glass in the
other, while Isabella stared blankly ahead. All that broke
the interminable silence was the slush of wine from de-
canter to glass at regular intervals which eventually wore
her ladyship's nerves to breaking point.

"Gideon," she protested at last, "don't you think you've
had enough?"

"No!" was the immediate reply, as he drained the glass and promptly replenished it again.

"But you must keep a clear head! W-We are depending on you."

"And this," he informed her, indicating the array of alcoholic beverages at his elbow, "is what I depend on."

To the Duke's surprise, she did something she had not done since she was a small child—she ran down the room and pitched herself on to his knee, flinging her arms around his neck for him to comfort her.

"Oo-oh, Gideon," she wailed into his shoulder. "Rosalind isn't . . . g-going to . . . to . . . d-die?"

"Of course not, 'Bella," he endeavoured to reassure her —yet nurturing grave doubts himself,

"Then why are you overwrought?"

"I am not overwrought!"

"You are—your nerves are shot to pieces! I've never seen you like this before—"

"Well, it's no thanks to me she isn't lying up there with her head blown off! When I fortuitously arrived she was actually sitting alone in the company of that accursed woman!"

"B-But I thought she was her mother?"

"Precisely! I tremble to think what Eugenia could have done before I came on the scene."

"Eugenia!" exclaimed her ladyship, beginning to see daylight. "Wasn't that the name of the woman you once —er—"

"Quite!" cut in the Duke, loth to hear the word mentioned.

"Rosalind's mother—fancy that!" gasped Isabella, stricken with awe. "Well I do declare! I see it all now—

I-I mean, why you brought her to live here an-and everything. . . ."

A lengthy pause followed whilst she digested this amazing discovery, to murmur anon: "How strange that we should encounter her the way we did, Gideon. . . ."

"Strange indeed, 'Bella—strange indeed."

The Duke could almost hear her mind ticking over in competition with the china ornamental clock behind them.

"Why did Rosalind's mother hate her so?" came the enquiry he was expecting.

"I believe, because she was jealous—"

"Jealous?" ejaculated Isabella, sitting bolt upright to view him askance. "What on earth had she to be jealous about? Surely she didn't think you were in love with Rosalind?"

"It—er—would appear so."

An even longer pause ensued, the Duke steeling himself for her next question.

"Y-You are not in love with her, are you, G-Gideon?"

He threw her a look of contempt. "How could I possibly love someone who is a constant reminder of all I wish to forget?"

"Er—exactly," she supported, without conviction, tracing imaginary patterns on his shoulder with a dimpled forefinger. "However, Gideon . . . d-don't you like her—j-just a little?"

"No, 'Bella."

"But you don't actually hate her, do you?"

"Most intensely!"

"Don't humbug me, Gideon!" she cried pettishly.

"Then mind your own affairs!" he flung back at her. "It doesn't signify because you are about to dash into wedlock, that I must follow suit! When will you realise that I am perfectly content with my present arrangements?"

He rose abruptly to his feet, precipitating her to the floor with a bump, going on to advise her that her time would be better expended in bed, replenishing her strength. To this, she was willing to consent on condition that he did likewise within the hour.

Isabella's solicitude for her brother's welfare was not in vain, and one gravely doubts if she would have slept quite so peacefully above had she cherished suspicions of what was happening down below—as the Duke sat drinking himself into oblivion. But although he drank heavily, by the early hours he was still in command of his senses, unable to banish the memory of that gruelling scene with its tragic end.

Upstairs, meanwhile, all was quiet as the maid sat by Rosalind's bed, supposedly keeping watch though her head drooped in evidence that she gently dozed—to start suddenly as the grandfather clock in the hall boomed out the hour of two. But even before the second chime had died away she was nodding again, unaware that the door had soundlessly opened. However, it did not close in like manner, and forcing open an eye to investigate, the girl shot off her chair in alarm at the unexpected sight of her employer, hastily straightening apron and cap as she bobbed a dutiful curtsy.

The Duke dismissed her with a curt nod—which she did not dare gainsay—and he remained by the door until the sound of her footsteps had died away. Only then did he venture over to the bed, to find Rosalind exactly as she had looked earlier—pale and helpless, the rise and fall of her bosom no more discernible.

Despite his inward revulsion, the Duke forced himself

to gaze upon his handiwork—upon this beautiful but fragile ghostly figure—immortal, except for the undeniable human evidence staining the snowy bandage swathing her head—and equally compelled his mind to plumb the very depths of her suffering as a form of penance, seeking to ease the intolerable burden of his conscience. For the first time in his life he found himself unable to reason situation or thoughts rationally. Only a matter of weeks ago his sole aim in life had been vengeance, well aware of the danger it courted—why, then, should he now doubt his action— why should he feel burdened with guilt, and the possibility of her death disturb him so acutely, as if he and not her mother had actually fired the shot? Why should he care— he, the infamous Delvray, whose name was a by-word for every vice and corruption—renowned for the unique depraved methods he devised for relieving his boredom? Why—when he had never harboured an ounce of decency in his entire being?

The Duke wiped a hand across his forehead, trying to rid himself of the guilt consuming his soul, and turning away from the bed, wandered over to the window to gaze out into the night, surveying with sightless eyes the moonlit gardens. Thus he stood, neither sound nor movement issuing from him—or the one lying prone in the huge fourposter, equally oblivious to time as it slowly passed them by.

But presently there came a movement from the bed, as Rosalind became restive, her hand groping the rose-strewn coverlet, as if about to waken—but all this evoked from the Duke was a glance. Even when she made a few incoherent sounds and unleashed a loud groan, he merely eyed her a little longer. And though this was but a prelude to a chain of moans, fitful tossing and a cry or two, the

Duke would not be lured back—until his equanimity was dealt a shattering blow, but, strangely enough, not by any great effort on Rosalind's part. In fact, it was nothing but a ghost of a whisper on her tremulous lips which made him round from the window with every latent sense on the alert, to stare in a mixture of suspicion and disbelief at the bed, wondering if he had heard aright—when it came again, quite distinctly.

"G-Gid . . . eon. . . . Gi . . . de . . . on. . . ."

He shook himself irritably, doubting if he were as sober as he believed. Although it was odd in itself that she should make use of his name, it was more the way her voice caressed it that filled him with foreboding as he cautiously approached the bed, not daring to acknowledge the truth already gnawing at his heart—long before she confirmed it.

"Gi-Gideon . . . m-my dear . . . est l-love, wh-where . . . are . . . y-you?"

The Duke stood riveted to the spot, shaking his head, refusing to accept the evidence of his ears as he stared at her, his face distorted with horror, utterly stunned, speechless, until he could bear the sound of her voice no longer.

"No, child! No!" he cried out, vehemently. "Not me—anyone but me! Y-You can't—it-it's not possible!"

Unleashing a terrible oath, he sank down on the bed, burying his face in his hands, realising the futility in remonstrating with her in her present condition—to rise abruptly and pace round the room in torment.

'Why, on top of all else, had this catastrophic thing to happen?' he asked himself repeatedly. 'Of all the suitors prostrate at her feet, why in heaven's name had she to fall in love with me? What is the fatal attraction—my wealth —title—or is it simply a form of hero-worship in gratitude for all I have done?' He flung away from her to the other side of the room, shrugging aside these suppositions as he ran his long fingers through his hair. 'To think the mysterious amour should be myself! Hell and the devil!' he swore aloud. 'How could I have been so blind? To have actually sat in Vauxhall Gardens discussing it at length—giving her the benefit of my advice! Even suggesting I intercede with the gentleman on her behalf! How ludicrous could a situation be? Why didn't I realise? Damn it all! There weren't many rich titled men she knew so well!'

He gave up in despair, and reluctantly retraced his steps to the bedside to lower himself wearily on to the edge of it, listening with half an ear to her disjointed confessions.

"Oh . . . G-Gideon—h-how . . . could she . . . hurt you s-so? . . . Y-You, the . . . m-man I . . . I l-love?" She shivered violently. "M-My heart . . . ach-aches . . . an-and my . . . h-head . . ." She broke off, raising a trembling hand to the bandage.

The Duke cursed, pushing her damp hair back from her face, but again she became restless.

"Why d-does . . . he . . . h-hate m-me?"—her voice broke on a sob.

"Hate you?" exclaimed the Duke, forgetting her ears were deaf to his words. "Satan's death! I don't hate you, child!"

Tears coursed slowly down her cheeks, inspiring the thought to him if she really were asleep, as he gently brushed them aside.

"I-I'm so . . . w-weak," she went on, in a faint breath. "With . . . out him . . . l-life is . . . d-death—so . . . I will . . . d-die. . . ."

"No, Rosalind!" he burst out again, on impulse. "You

mustn't talk of dying! You are so young, beautiful, with everything to live for!"

But she rambled on, oblivious to his deprecations. ". . . sweet d-death. . . . I w-will . . . d-die, G-Gideon, to g-give . . . you . . . p-peace . . ."

"Death? Peace? What gibberish is this?"

". . . end your . . . s-suff . . . ering—no one . . . to remind you . . . you . . . of h-her. . . ."

"But you don't, child! Never in a thousand years!" he shouted, growing exasperated. " 'S Blood! You're nothing like her and never were! I must have been crazed to even think it!"

"P-Please, Gid . . . eon, f-for . . . give . . . me. . . ."

The Duke released a groan. "Forgive you! For what? 'Tis I who needs forgiveness—for the pain you now endure —for using your young sweet innocence as a vulnerable pawn in my evil game to snare the queen. What excuse can I offer? I can't swear I did not expect this to happen when I personally contrived it!"

Suddenly her raving ceased, leaving her strangely quiet. Though she was unaware of it, never had she looked more ravishingly desirable, in her pitiful weakness—her hair, like liquid silver in the mellow candlelight, cascading over the pillows, creating a glorious halo round the intoxicating beauty of her face.

The Duke, clasping her hand, remained tensed and silent, instinctively holding his breath as her eyelashes fluttered slightly—but her eyes stayed closed. Instead, he felt her fingers returning the pressure of his and she smiled wanly, apparently reassured.

'Does she know what she is saying—doing?' he wondered yet again. 'That I am actually here in person, and not just a figment of her feverish imagination?'

She raised the hand she held and pressed it to her wet cheek. "Good . . . bye, Gid . . . eon. P-Perhaps we . . . will m-meet . . . again. . . ."

His blood ran cold as her head fell helplessly to one side and her fingers went limp in his hand.

"Rosalind—come back!" he yelled, distracted, seizing her into his arms. "Damn you, woman—speak to me!"

The next crucifying moment, everything went black and the Duke felt his whole world reel madly as it ran out of control—yet he, with all his wealth and influence, was utterly powerless to stop it. All he could think to do as a last resort was offer up a prayer, and battled frantically to recall one from his childhood, to discover—alas—not only had he forgotten how to pray, but that he had no god to pray to—for how could he petition the one in heaven after serving the one in hell all his life? He felt himself falling—down, down, into the dark abysmal chasm of despair, to be engulfed and lost for ever, when a movement closer by suddenly bore him out of the abyss, back into the light.

Rosalind stirred in his arms and the Duke stared down at her in bewilderment, wondering how her lightly-clad semi-conscious form came to be there—wiping the perspiration from his brow with his free hand, further surprised to find himself actually trembling. How long had he sat here thus—one year—two?

She now slept peacefully, her breathing stronger and regular—but the Duke's conscience was at anything but peace as it fought against the forces of nature to gainsay the powerful feeling surging through his veins. At once, he sought to convince himself that the situation was no different to their plight in Vauxhall Gardens when he had comforted her in a similar way . . . though reluctantly admitted that it had not undermined his self-control to such an alarming degree.

However, he still strove manfully to deny its existence, forcing his eyes up to the brocade canopy overhead—the china water-jug on the dresser—the white bear skin rug on the floor—the furniture—the walls—ceiling—anything! Granted, there was plenty to distract his eyes, but nought to distract his senses from the feel of her soft voluptuous body through the thin silk gown—or the proximity of her lips which, on the night in question, had not bothered him in the least, let alone accelerated his heartbeat to twice its normal rate! Despite himself, he flashed a downward glance at her—neither had they seemed so delectably inviting. . . .

The Duke adhered rigidly to the belief that his weakness was due solely to his over-indulgence in the brandy, and once he had secured a good night's rest, things would appear vastly different.

And so, without disturbing her sleep, he tried to lay her back on the pillows. He was just about to congratulate himself on accomplishing this feat, when her head suddenly fell back on his arm, bringing her slightly parted lips perilously close—so close, in fact, that he could feel her delicate breath on his cheek. Before the Duke even had time to think—let alone reason the outcome of his action—his resistance collapsed in ruins and his lips were on hers, recklessly disregarding the dictates of his conscience.

The kiss was ardent but tender—until he felt her gradually rousing, coming alive in his arms in eager response to the electrifying thrill which had shot through her, when it flared into a blazing passion, evoking in her a frightening emotion too powerful to control.

Rosalind was drugged with desire, delirious, but this delirium had no connection with her illness, for she was wide-eyed and fully awake! This was no dream, it was wonderfully real! She no longer laboured under the belief that he was nought but a romantic phantom conjured up in her sick mind, for she could feel his arms, his lips, as she returned his fervid feeling in frenzied abandon. Her face, neck, shoulders, all flamed with his kisses, and her flesh tingled beneath his hands—and though her head throbbed painfully she did not care, but surrendered completely to his dangerous passion, wallowing in the rapture of it as he crushed her to him—the Duke insensible to all else except the excruciating longing for her consuming his being.

"Forgive me! Rosalind, forgive me!" he implored her at length, his voice hoarse with emotion. "I had no idea anything like this would happen! I swear, I should not have come—"

Their lips met again as Rosalind drew his head down, swimming in ecstasy and wanting it never to end, clinging to him, lest he vanish into the night like some enchanted prince.

Once reassured, her head fell on his shoulder and she seemed content to lie thus, cradled in his arms—a state of mind certainly not borne by the Duke, who was suffering the first pangs of remorse at taking such unfair advantage of her present weakness.

"I pray, in the name of all that's holy, you are too far gone, sweet child, to appreciate what has happened this night," he murmured in her ear, burying his face in the haven of her golden hair. "But whether you hear me or not, I promise on sacred oath I will not rest until I have atoned personally for all you have suffered. At this moment I consider myself lower than hell itself, and I must try thus to win back a particle of self-respect if I am to go on living and face what future I have left to me. I swear I will do all in my power to bring you the happiness you crave. You will have a wedding the envy of Society, and a husband who will worship you like the goddess you are—who will respect you—who will have riches enough to buy you your heart's every whim, and who will cherish you for the rest of your days! It is the very least you deserve! I give you my word, dear one, your life hence forward will prove a perfect example of wedded bliss with the man of your choice. I shall arrange it as soon as you are well. . . . Rosalind?"

There was no response, and glancing down the Duke found her asleep in his arms, her lips curling in a smile of sheer contentment.

"All you have to do, child, is recover your health," he whispered, laying her back on the pillows and brushing the bandage with his lips. "I will do the rest."

And as he softly quitted the room, a distant cock crowed lustily, heralding the dawn.

13

It was a perfect English September day, and Rosalind sat in the comforting shade of a huge rambling oak out of the sun's powerful glare, fanning herself wearily with the largest leaf she could find, wondering how even the birds found strength to sing so heartily on such a hot day. Two months had expired since the tragic day, and she was now quite recovered from her illness. Even the angry scar—which she at first thought she would be branded with for life—had faded to a pale pink.

Thus she sat, pensively chewing a blade of grass and wafting the leaf back and forth, not really perturbed about being left to her own devices, as she had a great deal weighing on her mind and would have found company (except that of the Duke) excessively irritating. Her father had already returned to his Sussex home—anxious not to impose upon the Duke's generous hospitality once his daughter was in good health again. And Isabella, assured that Rosalind could contrive without her, had accepted the kind invitation of her future mother-in-law, the Dowager Viscountess Sevington, to spend a few days at Dryden Manor, in order to become better acquainted with the elderly lady who suffered a leg affliction and was unable to venture far out of doors. As for the Duke, Rosalind—to her chagrin—knew nought of his whereabouts except that he was engaged upon his annual round of calls to friends retired to their country seats for the hunting and shooting. Since his one memorable visit during her illness she had not set eyes upon him, which, apart from the heartache it begot, struck her as rather peculiar for one supposedly enamoured of her.

She flung the oak leaf petulantly away, wondering why he did not return to clear up the vexed question of her future—and his own. He had promised on oath to wed her, and to honour her dearest wish—which at present was to see him, for him to take her in his arms again and confirm his love—even if he had not actually said so, or made any flowery worded declaration. No doubt he was aware at the time just how useless any such declaration would be in her state of indisposition and had postponed it to some future date when she would be able to appreciate the serious step he would want her to take.

'Even so,' she sighed, rising to shake the folds out of her lavender muslin and stroll down the grove between the tubs of orange trees, 'it was extremely odd for a man to so abandon the woman he loved and intended soon to marry.' She ambled to a halt by the edge of the lake, her gaze scanning the calm water for sign of life, but it was quite deserted, with not even a swan to bear her company. Nothing but the gigantic stone fountain playing in the centre, sculptured with naiades sporting armfuls of stone blossoms—all very elaborate, but very cold, and very, very dead.

She wandered on along the grassy bank, indifferent to her idyllic surroundings—the delightful birdsong complemented by the buzzing ostinato of the bees, to the underlying gentle lap-lapping of the water—until an unexpected sound intruded, and she drew herself up to listen. It was a low distant rumble—'Of thunder, perhaps?' instinct suggested, to be firmly rejected by reason, as her eye surveyed the blue cloudless heavens.

However, thunder or no, it prompted the decision to retrace her steps indoors where it would be refreshingly cooler, but on emerging from the orange grove her heart missed a beat, for there, stationed at the door, was the Duke's much travel-stained coach—the cause of the mysterious rumbling she had heard and not the threat of a thunderstorm after all.

The servants, busily unloading the baggage from the vehicle, stood respectfully aside to let her pass, and without sparing them a second glance, Rosalind proceeded through the door, across the palatial hall and up the grand staircase, battling inwardly to maintain her dignity and not break into a headlong gallop to her boudoir.

Throughout her painstaking toilette her heart palpitated wildly—anxious to look her very best after their lengthy separation, wondering if the Duke was experiencing the same excitement—trying to imagine how he would look . . . perhaps even more devastating than the great awe-inspiring portrait of him hanging in the long gallery, king over his never-ending line of supercilious ancestors, at which she gazed in silent homage each time she passed, held transfixed by those evil green eyes set in that pallid, handsome face, the sardonic curl of the lip expressing his insolent boredom, so peculiar to him, which the artist had captured to perfection. Yet, it was a ghost from the past, of the cruel being she had first encountered—not the man she had since grown to know and love, who had clutched her hungrily to him upon that vital night which now seemed so long ago, almost an eternity—but every single touch, kiss, caress he had bestowed and each word breathed into her delirious ear were printed indelibly on her mind.

But despite her meticulous preparation then, and upon

the succeeding days, Rosalind found to her desolation that her guardian seemed to prefer the seclusion of his private apartments to the prospect of her company, yet she never relinquished hope of a summons to his august presence, sitting up until almost midnight, waiting, struggling to keep awake, or often denying herself the pleasure of an exhilarating gallop across the downs lest he call and she not be on hand to answer. Instead, she would elect to wile away the hours upon the spinet, breezing through magazines, or adding a stitch or two to her tapestry—consoling herself in the knowledge that he was in the throes of a punctiliously worded speech designed to sweep her off her feet.

Nevertheless, her youthful exuberance finally began to flag, giving way to despair and bitterness, wondering what on earth he was doing, and not ready to admit that the idea of him concocting a proposal screamed of the ridiculous—for even Bart, as dull-witted as he was, could have worded twenty proposals in the last three days, let alone her singularly eloquent guardian!

It was upon the evening of the fourth day, howbeit, that her anxious wait came to an end. She sat in the music salon at the harpsichord, seeking to drown her turbulent emotions in a particularly boisterous piece which suited her mood admirably. With a thunderous chord which shook the room she finished the piece and abandoned the instrument to flop face down on an adjacent day-bed, where she law sprawled disconsolately, the hoop of her sugar-pink taffeta gown sticking up at an odd angle as she stared the pattern off the thick Turkish carpet, whilst mentally reviewing her hopeless plight.

"Permit me to commend your performance," sounded the Duke's voice, close at hand.

Rosalind shot up erect, hastily straightening her gown, her face turning a variety of colours as her eye alighted on his elegant figure reclining in a chair less than six feet away.

"It has improved considerably since your arrival here," he went on indifferently, as if not really bothered whether it had or not, whilst his eyes, veiled by heavy lids, vainly scanned his already impeccable person for sign of a flaw. "Methinks I now detect an element of harmony—as if your hands had finally reached a compromise."

"Th-thank you, your Grace," she stammered, not really sure if it were meant to be a compliment, wondering how long he had sat thus obtruding upon her privacy, appreciating that her exceptionally loud playing must have drowned the sound of his entrance.

"I do not seek to interrupt. Pray continue an you so wish." He gestured briefly towards the instrument.

"S-Somehow I've lost the inclination," she responded breathlessly, clasping her hands firmly to still their trembling, wishing she could quell her wild heartbeat as easily.

How incredibly strange, after enduring weeks of unbearable torment, yearning frantically to see him, she now found it an utter impossibility to even look in his direction. And instead of throwing herself eagerly into his arms as she had envisaged, she was seized with embarrassment and blushed like some simple schoolroom chit, certain that he must surely hear her heart pounding madly, as it dinned in her ears, telling her that this was it—the moment she had been languishing for! He was here—had sought her out purposefully! There could be only one reason!

"You are well, I trust?" he enquired of a sudden, as it occurred to him.

"Perfectly well, thank you!" she replied sprightly, to

assure him that she was quite ready to receive his proposal, no matter how wildly amorous.

"And your health fully restored?"

"Completely!"

Having established this, he rose to his feet, impatiently flicking a non-existent crease from the whale-boned skirt of his azure silk coat ere he proceeded to stroll about the room, gazing abstractedly round the fine collection of instruments—while Rosalind perched agitatedly on the daybed, casting surreptitious glances at him through her lashes in an effort to define his mood.

'Rather austere,' she thought, 'for a man contemplating the joyous prospect of wedlock.'

"I now consider the moment opportune, Miss Tremayne—"

'Miss Tremayne!' she gasped inwardly. 'How dreadfully formal!'

"—to discuss a rather intimate matter," he went on, somewhat curtly. "During your illness, I made a certain promise which—as you laboured 'neath delirium at the time—you may not recall, or indeed even be aware of. However, to phrase it in simple terms," he hurried on, granting her no chance to confirm or deny it, "I took it upon myself to guarantee your future happiness through marriage with the man of your choice, whomsoever he happened to be."

Rosalind's eyes followed him round the room, her former diffidence forgotten as she noticed a marked change in him—not only a difficulty in selecting his words, but his inability to stand in one place, instead roaming constantly about, his brows creased deep in thought—so alien to his nature, up and down, back and forth, as if searching for something but unable to decide precisely what, preserving the while a distance between she and himself of ten feet or so.

"I would therefore inform you that I now find myself in a position to fulfil my promise," he announced stiffly, as if quoting an official document. "With your co-operation, of course."

'At least the introduction was original,' she silently approved, as he turned to query an afterthought.

"I presume marriage is still your objective?"

She nodded encouragingly, staring up at him, but his eyes fluttered away, unable to meet her gaze.

'Who is this stranger?' Rosalind asked herself, stunned, 'this tensed, disturbed man, wringing his hands behind him, unable to look me in the eye.' Had he been some immature lovesick swain, well could she have understood! But her guardian? What had become of that languid non-chalance so much a part of him—that indomitable wit—most of all, that overall air of sheer imperturbability?

This, she was certainly not prepared for! Why should a simple proposal of marriage prove such a formidable task to one so disgustingly self-assured? Surely he did not anticipate rejection?

He finally halted by the fireplace with his back to the cold empty grate, his eyes fixed on some distant point beyond the windows opposite—and if conscious of her determined efforts to catch his eye, was equally determined that she should not.

"Is there any particular quality you desire in a husband?" he saw fit to resume.

Rosalind was more puzzled than ever. "Isn't it rather late to be asking such a question, your Grace?"

"On the contrary—now is the time to weigh all aspects of the matter before it is too late," he returned frigidly.

" 'Tis not much use complaining once the ring is on your finger, should he happen to brandish a wooden leg."

"A wooden leg!" she retorted, piqued by his attitude. "I must say, you manage to conceal it extremely well!"

The Duke raised his eyes ceilingwards, inhaling a deep breath to help restore his mental equilibrium.

"Obviously, Miss Tremayne, I was not referring to myself."

"Whom then, may I ask, were you referring to?"

At last, he allowed his eyes to travel to her face, regarding her strangely. "Whom but the man you are destined to wed?"

A deathly hush fell as confused blue eyes stared up into equally confused green—neither daring to acknowledge what the other was thinking.

"I-I don't quite understand," whispered Rosalind, about to faint with horror at the thought which was battling for supremacy in her mind.

The Duke swung round to the fireplace, unable to meet the accusation in her eyes. "I-I'm sorry, Rosalind," he murmured, almost inaudibly. "There appears to have been some misunderstanding."

"Misunderstanding!" she echoed, stricken. "Perhaps you would deign to explain!"

He heaved a sigh of despair. "I don't know how much you remember of that ill-fated night—"

"Everything!"

"Impossible!" he contradicted. "You were ranting and raving like one possessed—"

"If I was possessed, Gideon, it was with you!" she retaliated, wretchedly. "How could I possibly remain unconscious when you were there—the man I loved—clasping me in your arms, and—"

"Spare me the crucifying details, I beg you!" he groaned
—shattering her heart.

"Forgive me if the reminder fills you with repugnance,"
she declared harshly, averting her eyes to hide the anguish
she knew was manifest. "At the time, despite my condition, I felt certain it was meant sincerely—evidently I was
mistaken about that, too!"

"In heaven's name, child! Must you continue racking
me?" he burst out violently. "You know damned well you
weren't deceived—but the knowledge that it was meant
sincerely makes the burden no easier to bear! It should
never have happened! I lost my self-control and gave way
to weakness for which I shall despise myself eternally!"

Rosalind rounded on him, eyes flashing. "If your feelings
were genuine, why have you now gone back on your
word?"

"I wasn't aware I had!"

"What, then, would you term it, when you promise to
wed me then openly deny it?"

"I did not promise to wed you!" he thundered, incensed.
"You misconstrued my meaning. I assure you, I meant
every word of the pledge I gave you—and still do—but I
am not, and never was, part of the bargain!"

Rosalind's bitter disappointment gave way to contempt,
believing him to be simply seeking a means of escape. "Did
you, or did you not, my Lord Duke, promise I should
marry the man of my choice?" she challenged, wither-
ingly.

"Agreed—but what woman in command of her senses
would wish to wed a man who had used her so abominably
—who had deliberately sought her downfall and ruin—
and almost caused her death?"

"I do not hold you responsible for my mother's actions.

Furthermore, as you were by then aware that the man I loved was none other than yourself, surely it must have occurred to you who my obvious choice would be?"

The Duke flung up his hands in defeat. "Alas—no. I'm afraid it did not," he admitted, ruefully. "The very idea is too absurd for any sane being to contemplate."

The unbearable silence returned to blanket the atmosphere, the Duke wandering about the room visibly overwrought, the dictates of his conscience wrestling with his emotions, until—regaining some of his customary composure—he trusted himself to venture a little nearer, and ultimately drew to a halt within reach of her. When next he spoke, his tone was compassionate.

"I promised you happiness, Rosalind—so far as it's in my power to give—not a living hell. I am too set in my licentiousness to transform miraculously overnight into the dutiful spouse you deserve. My own mother despaired of me long before she died, and if she failed, I cannot in all honesty see you succeeding. No, child," he went on, a note of finality in his voice. "You must choose one worthy of the honour you would bestow—someone pure of body and mind, who commands your respect—"

"I want to marry a full-blooded man, not an archbishop!" she rejoined, tartly.

"Why not compromise and accept one of your many admirers? I can arrange for them to begin calling this very week. You will be allowed ample time to make up your mind—"

"Stop! Stop!" she screamed, unable to endure any more hard calculating of her future. "I won't! I can't! You don't know what you're asking! You can't mean it—you can't!"

"Rosalind—please!"

"How can you even suggest it? How could I ever consider marrying anyone else, loving you as I do?" she besought him, her anguished eyes searching his face, frantically, for some sign—any sign—that he was about to relent—but, alas, in vain.

Instead, he sank down beside her, and gently took her hands in his, now in his role as guardian, realising she was not going to be easily dissuaded.

"Child," he began, his gaze riveted on the hands he held. "No one regrets what has happened more bitterly than I. Believe me, I would give anything for our paths never to have crossed. I was so blinded by my own selfish desire for vengeance, I simply refused to entertain the possibility that it might all rebound on me by falling on the innocent head of one I have grown to . . . to . . . honour and admire above all. If only there were something I could do! I swear, I would willingly sacrifice the rest of my worthless life to spare you the pain which must be yours. . . ." He bent his head and kissed her hands with reverence. "It may comfort you to know, Rosalind—you do not suffer alone."

He raised his eyes to hers and she choked back a sob as she drank in the agony of soul manifest in their green depths, realising at once that whatever burden she would bear in future, his would be ten times the greater.

"Oh, why, Gideon? Why?" she whispered, brokenly. "Why inflict this terrible punishment on us both?"

"Would you have me inflict a worse punishment on you —by making you my wife?" he countered, caustically, releasing her hands.

"Yes! Yes! If you are bent on self-persecution, then at least grant me the happiness you promised."

"Rosalind—I beg you!" he implored, desperately.

"Don't add to my wretchedness by stripping me of the only shred of decency I have left. Please allow me to do what I believe is right."

He would have risen, but she seized his arm to make one last bid to save her future.

"Gideon! I refuse to believe you are indifferent to me—the way you . . . you . . . k-kissed me—"

"I had been drinking heavily—I-I was not responsible for my actions!" he cut in to vindicate himself.

"B-But I worship you!" she pleaded, forcing down the lump in her throat threatening to take possession of her. "Knowing this, how can you condemn me in marriage to someone else?"

"There is no alternative," he returned brusquely, prising her rigid fingers from his huge silver-embroidered cuff and mounting resolutely to his feet. "You must!"

"I can't! It's impossible! You're demanding too much of me!"

"You can and will!"

"But you love me! I know you do!"

"My feelings are my own personal concern and have no bearing whatsoever on the issue!" he rasped irritably, his patience wearing thin as he laboured 'neath the strain of his convictions.

"What about my feelings?" cried Rosalind, renewing her attack, also leaping afoot. "Don't they matter either?"

"You are young—you will soon overcome this childish infatuation with your guardian—perhaps even laugh over it in years to come."

"And you, my Lord Duke?" she flashed, scornfully. "Will you also laugh?"

He stopped dead, to round on her. "Why not?" he

snarled with blistering sarcasm. "Isn't it all hysterically amusing?"

"I've no doubt your companions at White's will find it so—a juicy morsel indeed, for them to make meat of!"

The whole room seemed about to explode as they stood confronting each other, Rosalind's eyes smouldering with rancour at him, while the Duke's blazed furiously at her.

"I presume this to be a sample of your personal atonement for all I've endured on your behalf," she snorted.

He winced as her arrow hit its mark, but managed to rein in his temper. "I shall atone by uniting you in marriage to any man you wish—anyone! Just name him! Any man in the entire world!"

"Except yourself!" she sneered, peeved at the humiliation she was suffering after baring her heart to him so rashly. "Very well!" she declared, stifling her broken heart beneath a cloud of disdain as she rose to her full height, to stagger him with her announcement. "I will wed the Earl of Alnstone within the month!"

The Duke stiffened. "Even if you meant it, you know as well as I that it's out of the question."

"Why? You asked me to name a man and I've named one!"

"You are understandably distraught and need time to adjust—"

"I will marry Lord Alnstone!" she screamed, stubbornly.

"It is customary to wait for a proposal!" he hurled back.

Rosalind choked down her rage, her bosom heaving. "Have him call as soon as possible," she hissed through her teeth, "then kindly make the necessary wedding arrangements."

"As you wish!" snapped the Duke, his temper showing through at last. "But if you think to spite me by marrying the first man to languish at your feet, you're galloping up the wrong road!"

She cast him a scathing glance, strangling her fingers with the blue velvet ribbon adorning her gown. "As I cannot marry for love, I shall marry for the next best thing—wealth!" she stated cuttingly. "He is monstrous rich, I hear—so I shall follow your good example and devote my life entirely to pleasure, casually treading upon any who have the ill-fortune to get in my way."

"So—we're hell-bent on self-destruction, just like your mother?"

"Exactly like my mother!" she flared, hammering the last nail in her coffin. "She knew what life was about! Perhaps if I'd been more like her, things might have been very different between us."

"What precisely do you mean by that?" he demanded, eyeing her dangerously.

"I mean that my mother didn't do too badly for herself, upon reflection—for not only was she given a proposal of marriage, but the comfort of your bed, to boot!"

No sooner were the words airborne than Rosalind realised her mistake—she had gone too far! Her impetuous tongue had finally proved her downfall, and with it her courage evaporated leaving her trembling like a willow branch—as the Duke exploded.

"Get out! Hell and the devil, get out—before I do something I will deucedly regret!"

Not waiting for a second command, Rosalind was off—through the hall and up the stairs with his thunderous voice echoing in her ears, as he snatched up a delicate porcelain figurine of the god of pastures green, and roared: "Follow her and be damned!"—before Pan and his merry pipes were sent shattering against the nearest wall.

14

The Duke lost no time in fulfilling his ward's explicit request, and the following Friday afternoon saw the bewildered Earl of Alnstone being ushered into the white drawing-room at Claremont Park, in response to an invitation from the Duke to expend a day or two at his Wiltshire home—but sounding suspiciously like a command and which the Earl, had he so wished, would have thought twice about refusing. But it was not until he was firmly established in the house that he was given to understand the reason for his abrupt summons, which left him bereft of speech for the remainder of the day, and had he been called upon to declare himself that evening, would have experienced no little difficulty in making any coherent sound.

Indeed, Lord Alnstone—a slender gentleman of average height, with a capacity to please when not submerged beneath a torrent of bombastic acclamations (made to draw attention to his wealth and position, and away from his deficiencies in size, personality, and wit)—could hardly believe his good fortune, that Rosalind actually favoured his suit, for she certainly had not given him that impression at their last meeting when, he was still convinced, she had evaded him quite deliberately.

Many damsels had been attracted by his reasonable good looks and handsome fortune, but despite these valuable assets, those worth paying court to usually lost interest rather quickly on account of his poor sense of humour and sharp temper. Only very deep down did he grudgingly acknowledge his awkwardness with the fair sex, his lack of charm and honeyed blandishments, necessary in the repertoire of the gay seducer—but now appreciated how grossly he had been underestimating his appeal, and hiding his light 'neath the proverbial bushel.

His morale thus boosted, the Earl prepared himself for his meeting with a surfeit of confidence, spending several hours with his man, prinking and preening himself, haresfoot in one hand, curling-tongs in the other, suffering his head to be submerged in the powder-bag no less than three times (inducing an avalanche of sneezes) and his torso constricted by his whaleboned corset (which he trusted would not be detected) a further two inches—all to impress upon his lady-love what a dashing handsome fellow he was and how exceedingly fortunate she should deem herself in securing his attentions, whilst inwardly applauding himself at being selected from the long line of contenders for her hand. But, alas, the time wasted on his appearance would have been better spent feeding the swans on the lake, for the notice Rosalind took of his immaculate cream brocade coat, rainbow waistcoat, and elegantly powdered locks—and the fact that he was sprayed from head to toe in a devastating new scented toilet water called 'L'Homme Fatal'.

The Duke and the Earl spent the entire Sunday morning closeted with their respective lawyers and men of business to draw up the marriage contract, which was finally signed and sealed by noon. A light repast ensued for those inclined to eat, and at two in the afternoon the actual betrothal took place, which must surely have been registered in the archives as the briefest and frostiest in history! True, the Earl had been granted little time to compose a lengthy speech extolling his virtues, but even so, would have had much ado to deliver it. Instead, he made his proposal, was frigidly accepted, placed the diamond-and-ruby ring upon her finger in exchange for which Rosalind reluctantly presented her cold left cheek for him to kiss—and it was all over.

Afterward, the Earl thought it strange enough that no celebration in any shape or form was to take place, but when his affianced of five minutes' standing swept off to her boudoir pleading a piercing headache, and his host to the study to drink himself to death, leaving him to his own amusement, he considered it bordering on insult—especially when he found himself obliged to endure the billing and cooing of the Lady Isabella and Lord Sevington, who —so rapt in each other—remained oblivious to his presence throughout the afternoon.

However, to his immense satisfaction, following the betrothal the situation was not allowed to stagnate, and arrangements were at once set in motion for the wedding, to take place in London on October 20th—the earliest possible date, being a mere five weeks away. Orders were dispatched to the Duke's aunt to be placed with florists, jewellers, and other merchants, together with an invitation list as long as a church spire, and a request for her to have available a wide selection of suitable materials for his ward's perusal on their arrival the following week.

The discovery that they were all to journey to London so soon for her wedding confused Rosalind's emotions even more, and she experienced her first pangs of genuine misgiving, conscious of the nuptial net gradually closing round her and that she had no choice but to go through with it, for the Duke was now desperate to get her out of his house, and furthermore, she was every bit as desperate to go. Thus obliged to marry someone, she found the Earl as eligible as any other, and richer by far! Both she and her father would wallow in luxury for the rest of their lives.

But by the time London was reached she was not nearly so confident. To say the journey had proved a sore trial would be a howling understatement, for throughout she had found herself confined in one coach with Betty, her personal maid, and her future husband—obliged to endure his odious advances, tiresome compliments (more to himself than she) as he drivelled over her hand, his hot breath on her cheek and his unbearable nearness—whilst the Duke, Lord Sevington and Isabella occupied a second coach. That the intolerable arrangement had been deliberately engineered by the Duke, she did not doubt. To enjoy a brief respite when the road was quitted for the night was all that saved her sanity, and upon finally arriving at Cavendish Square she could have danced with joy—not only at escaping from Lord Alnstone, but to see her father, whom she had not expected to see quite so soon.

Two evenings later, a small dinner party was held in her honour by the Countess, also designed to bring Sir Roger and his future son-in-law together that they might become acquainted before the wedding. The company embraced close friends and relatives—the Duke's chair significantly vacant, having declined his aunt's invitation on some flimsy pretext, thus provoking her feminine curiosity and setting the cogs of her nimble mind in motion.

A mountain of preparation gave a powerful spurt to the following two weeks, for in addition to the wedding there was to be a dazzling wedding-eve ball given by the Countess, not only in honour of the marriage, but to celebrate the long-awaited betrothal of her adored niece, Isabella and Lord Sevington. The wedding breakfast was to be given—to Rosalind's further humiliation—by the Duke himself at his own town-house, which she acknowledged his culminating insult!

During this time, Lord Alnstone was, understandably, a frequent visitor at Cavendish Square, dancing attendance on his future bride and proving a veritable thorn in her delicate flesh—so much so that Rosalind welcomed the arrival of the following week with more than reasonable enthusiasm, which she was to spend at Tremayne Grange with her father—asking herself how on earth she was to endure the rest of her life with the Earl when a mere half-hour of his company drove her to distraction. It was not so much the gentleman himself she found so excessively oppressive—she readily agreed that she would feel the same irritation with any other—except one, the one she loved, whom she had not seen since her arrival in London, but whom she yet hoped would call and beg her to change her mind and marry him instead—or even call to give her a chance to crave his forgiveness. And when she arrived at Tremayne Grange that subsequent weekend, her hopes of seeing the Duke still prevailed, praying he would come and seek her out.

The old house in Sussex was a wonderful change— pleasantly serene, conducive to her mood, allowing her time to delve into her conscience in search of an alternative means of solving her predicament.

Meanwhile, Sir Roger quietly observed his daughter— indeed, had been observing her for some time. Her extreme reluctance to discuss her future husband struck him as rather peculiar, for most young maids could talk of nought else! All he received in response to his paternal enquiries were monosyllables, and he was positively taken aback by her many bouts of megrims and tears which she tried to justify as pre-wedding nerves. At first he accepted this as plausible, but by the end of the week was perilously near to suspecting the truth. Even so, he cherished his suspicions to himself in the hope that she would anon venture the information without any coercion on his part. Despite his life of seclusion, Sir Roger knew a deal more than others gave him credit for—including all the obvious signs of unrequited love. Whom, then, was she in love with? Evidently not her future husband!

However, the week finally drew to a close without Rosalind making any attempt to unburden herself to her father, and, furthermore, trusted she had thrown him off the scent with her feeble excuses, for she had no intention of unburdening her heart to anyone—certainly not following her last experience with the Duke, who was the only person in the world who could save her from her fate in seven days. She would be back in London the next day— there was still time for him to grant her a reprieve.

But back in Cavendish Square the atmosphere was unbearable as last-minute preparations for the wedding got under way and everyone fussed feverishly round her. Wedding gifts were arriving by the gross and every five minutes she was being prevailed upon to have some gown or other fitted—apart from visitors dropping in by the dozen whom she was obliged to entertain, indulging their eagerness for wedding chatter by forcing an enthusiasm she found gruelling to summon. Indeed, it would seem that every single inhabitant of London called at Cavendish Square during that last week, except the one person she still yearned madly to see and kept constant vigil for by the window through the day—escaping to the haven of her boudoir at night, on any pretext, unaware that her strange conduct was being remarked with growing concern by her father and the Countess, who tut-tutted to themselves, exchanging dubious glances as they slowly despaired of the situation. And they were not alone in their anxiety. The Earl himself began to harbour doubts about his fiancée's health which had suddenly become a trifle too delicate for his peace of mind, and the many fine sons he was anticipating her bearing him, to extend his noble line.

Eventually, the wedding eve arrived, most of which Rosalind passed in her room 'resting', striving to rally sufficient courage to face everyone—including the Duke who was certain to be present—wondering if on this, the last night of her life, he would bring himself to speak to her—perhaps even ask her to dance—or spirit her away from this terrible nightmare. Oh, agony of agonies! However was she to survive the ordeal on the morrow, knowing he was there in the church witnessing her execution?

Throughout her toilette—a mechanical ritual—Rosalind felt more like a mummy being embalmed for the tomb, phlegmatically tolerating the perpetual fussing of Aunt Gertrude and her battalion of maids, whilst Isabella danced round and round her, delirious with joy over her imminent engagement. Even the donning of her beautiful ball gown made entirely of silver thread and worn over the most gigantic hoops available did nothing to raise her spirits from the depths of despondency.

When she at last descended the stairs escorted by the captivated Earl, poignant memories, which were to recur throughout the evening, surged back of her presentation ball and how she had floated down the self-same stairs on the arm of the Duke. And as she entered the glittering ballroom—the same guests, in the same hues of silks, satins and brocades, the same chandeliers shining down on the scene—everything exactly the same, except the man by her side whom she was to wed on the morrow, and who thrilled her as wildly as a platterful of cold pottage.

She could vaguely remember being led out to commence the ball—a cold marble statue, impervious to the gasps of admiration she evoked from the gathering assembled around the room, or that they represented the cream of Society.

The evening wore on, Rosalind dancing with Lord This and the Honourable That, all familiar faces, but none the face she sought. Not once had she glimpsed the Duke but she knew he was there somewhere, for according to his aunt (who had loudly commented to a guest, in Rosalind's hearing)—'He does not look at all well—quite unlike Gideon, for he has never suffered a day's illness in his life!' Rosalind had felt a pang of alarm, but at the same time an ember of hope had kindled within, that maybe—was it possible?—she herself was the cause.

Yet again she was obliged to dance with her husband-to-be, each dance a greater trial than the last, the clasp of his hot clammy hands, his suffocating breath on her face, and the way he clutched her to him at every opportunity, as if fearing she might disappear before his eyes. On and on she danced, her amorous fiancé palling her more and more, the atmosphere growing hotter and hotter, mingled with his heady perfume—until her head suddenly reeled as if she was about to faint.

"P-Please!—Please, t-take me . . . to the g-gardens . . . a-at once," she besought the Earl, weakly.

Lord Alnstone beamed like a child promised a special treat, and before she could blink, bore her off towards the gardens with such alacrity that her feet hardly touched the floor. But out in the secluded shadows of the shrubbery, Rosalind soon discovered the underlying reason for his enthusiasm as he seized her passionately in his arms, moist lips at the ready to devour her with kisses. Overcome with nausea, she struggled frantically to free herself, unable to endure him any longer. But the Earl's arms grew tighter and tighter until she could scarce breathe—her head spinning madly as frenzied horrifying visions of what she must suffer on her wedding night flashed before her eyes.

"No! No! Never!" she screamed at last, pushing him off with revulsion. "I can't! I can't!"

"What d'ye mean, ye can't?" he rasped, enraged, battling to control himself.

"P-Please, my lord—I-I feel a little f-faint. . . . Be good enough to p-procure me . . . some c-cordial—water . . . anything—"

"Egad! Not another attack of y'r vapours!" he exclaimed, angrily. "What ails you, woman? All these headaches and attacks of this and that—you were never prone to such! I begin to suspect your convenient spasms nothing more than some clever ruse to keep me at arm's length!"

"P-Please . . . w-water. . . . I feel f-faint . . ." she gasped, ready to fake a fit—anything, to be rid of him.

He stood awhile, smouldering, then with an angry snort stalked away to fulfil her request.

Before he was out of sight, Rosalind sped off through the garden, determined he should not easily find her on his return. Fortunately, there were not many guests about, as the betrothal of Isabella and her Viscount was due to be announced in ten minutes, and the majority had returned indoors to witness the event. She hurried on down the

gardens, past the fishpond where she had suffered a similar
indignity with Sir Francis—on through the rockery, until
she came to the Chinese summer-house, tucked away in the
farthest corner amongst the trees, unknown to many—a
rambling glass structure with a tall pagoda-style dome,
which was how it had earned its name.

Here, Rosalind sought refuge, grateful to be alone at
last, able to cast aside her mask of affectation and be
free—free to give licence to her innermost feelings, and to
the wretchedness enveloping her heart.

She stood motionless, staring blankly through the glass,
numb with grief at her impending doom, wondering what
had possesed her to demand Lord Alnstone for a husband,
and how she was going to endure his repugnant love-
making. A shiver of horror ran through her body as she
compared him with the man she loved, recalling that rapturous night as she had countless times before, reliving
each impassioned moment anew. Even yet, she awoke in
the night dreaming he was there—so vividly she could
actually feel his arms, his hands, his lips! But from
tomorrow, a dream was all it would ever be—a sweet,
sweet memory—for he would no longer be her guardian,
and Claremont Park no longer her home. . . .

Tears began to flow down her cheeks at all the wonderful things she would miss—but most of all the owner, and
the little intimacies they had shared. She pressed her
burning forehead against the cool, cool glass, her tears
streaming down the pane.

"Oh, Gideon! Spare me this unbearable anguish! Save
me from this dreadful fate!" she sobbed wildly. "I can't
become the chattel of another man—I belong to you! I
shall always belong to you. . . ." She clung to the wooden
frame, her nails biting into it, fighting to quell the upsurge

of grief inside her. "How can I let another take what is rightfully yours? I-I love . . . you. . . . Gideon. . . ." She broke off, sobbing with agony of soul as she finally gave way to the misery rending her heart.

But Rosalind was not alone. In her bitter distress she failed to hear a step and slight movement behind, not realising anyone was there until a silk handkerchief was proffered, and she felt hands—gentle but firm—on her bare shoulders. Her first reaction was to turn and view the intruder, but the grip instinctively tightened, preventing her.

Even so, it was a familiar touch—she knew those hands.

"G-Gideon?" she ventured, breathlessly.

An excruciating silence followed, but she already knew it was he before he answered.

"Yes." It was something between a moan and a murmur.

A dry sob racked her in a mixture of relief and desire, as she closed her eyes, luxuriating in the strong clasp of his fingers.

"Have y-you for-forgiven m-me?"

"For what?"

"The t-terrible things I s-said . . . a-at Claremont P-Park."

"Don't—I beg you!" he pleaded, hoarsely. "How I have since rued that day—reproached myself constantly. . . ."

"Oh, Gideon!" she petitioned him, her very soul in her voice. "Won't you change your mind?"

He unleashed a groan of pure wretchedness. "I-It's no use, Rosalind . . . it's too late. . . ."

"No! No! There is still time! W-We could run away— tonight!"

"You would never survive the scandal."

"Scandal? Why should I care—if I belonged to you? And if I vanished overnight—or killed myself—wouldn't it be a scandal just the same?"

"Child! You can't—"

"You're right, Gideon! I can't—can't go through with it!"

His hold relaxed on her shoulders and as she swung round to confront him he stepped back into the shadows.

"I am weak, helpless—not strong and resilent like you —able to change your moods and feelings like you do your fashionable clothes!" Her voice caught on a sob. "Don't throw away our only chance of happiness. Is it to be the end of everything—the end of your noble line? Oh, Gideon," she battled on, clutching his arm in desperation. "Am I never to know the depth of your love—be borne away out of this miserable existence by your wild turbulent passion—never again feel the touch of your hands . . . y-your lips?"

"Rosalind!" he burst out in torment, flinging away from her to the door. "You're crucifying us both! It's impossible —quite impossible!"

"You want me to marry the Earl?" she cried out in anguish.

The Duke uttered a round curse. "What am I supposed to respond to that?"

"The simple truth!"

There was a lengthy pause before he slowly turned to gaze down on her despite his firm resolve not to, his gaunt haggard features and dark sunken eyes proclaiming his suffering, his sleepless nights and lack of sustenance over the past weeks.

"No," he sighed, burdened with remorse. "I do not want you to wed him, or anyone else—until the master craftsman comes along, able to mould you into the perfect woman you are destined to be—not some heavy-handed oaf who lets your breathtaking beauty fly to his head and defiles—your innocence beyond repair, merely to satisfy his own selfish canine appetite."

Rosalind stared up at him, compassion and adoration radiating from her eyes, glistening with tears—as if he were some god, or high priest, and she his sacrificial virgin—held transfixed by his devouring gaze as he finally drank his fill of her intoxicating face—framed by her glorious hair, elaborately styled in the height of fashion with two long ringlets—silver in the moonlight—wending their way over the graceful curve of one lily-white shoulder, down to nestle between her full rounded breasts—dangerously tempting as they protruded, pulsating, above the neck of her low-cut gown. Never had she looked more disturbingly beautiful—even more so than that disastrous night by her bed when he had fallen victim to her spell.

"Gideon?" she whispered at length, wishing to preserve the magical aura.

"Y-Yes?" he gasped.

"If I must still go through with it—the m-marriage, I mean—after a while, w-would you . . ." she broke off, bit her lip, then tried again, ". . . would you . . . be-become my . . . l-lover?"

This was the ultimate—the dagger in his side! With a groan of defeat he fell helplessly against the doorpost, eyes closed.

"Gideon! Please!—I-I'm desperately sorry!" she besought him, frantically, lest she had ruined her slender chance of ever winning him. "F-Forgive me!—I-I didn't mean to insult you—"

The dam burst! The emotional flood he had managed to

hold back now swept through him like a tornado as—to Rosalind's stupefied joy—he wrenched her into his arms, crushing her to him with insane desire, his mouth seeking hers with an insatiable hunger to release the explosion of passion surging in his veins, welding them together, kiss after feverish kiss proving his overwhelming love, his lips and hands continually craving for her as if his dire need would never be assuaged—their intense love for each other merging into one blazing furnace, engulfing them in its flames.

Thus, they relinquished themselves each to the other in reckless abandon, oblivious of all—including a ballroom of some thousand guests who were growing restive concerning the whereabouts of the Duke and the betrothal announcement he was due to have made fifteen minutes ago, wondering amongst themselves what could be more important to him than the engagement of his own sister and closest friend?

But the distinguished gathering experienced no greater anxiety than Lord Alnstone who had suddenly lost his bride-to-be, and having thoroughly scoured house and gardens to no avail, now solicited the aid of his hostess, who readily agreed to join him in the search—once she had prevailed upon Sir Roger to fill the breach and make the necessary announcement in place of her nephew.

It was not until the Countess was descending the five shallow steps into the gardens, accompanied by the Earl, that she began fitting the final pieces into her mental jig-saw puzzle—her nephew's agreement to distract Rosalind's affections—his recent reluctance to call at Cavendish Square, and trumped-up excuse to evade the party—his strained, tired look—coupled with Rosalind's sudden 'decline in health'—the guilt which consumed her at mention of his name, and most of all, the significance in the fact that they were the only two people missing at this crucial hour.

An ominous feeling germinated within her which developed with the search—the summer-house eventually occurring to her as a likely spot, bethinking it dark, secluded and certain to pass unseen by most—even an irate impetuous Earl. As the Earl had taken himself off to search on the farther side, the Countess seized her chance and hastened off towards the summer-house. Drawing near, she hesitated with bated breath, listening for a sound, but all remained unnaturally quiet and so she tiptoed on, emerging from behind a bush to stop short, stricken at what met her eyes. For several seconds the Countess was speechless! She had stumbled upon lovers kissing many times in her life, but had witnessed nothing quite like the two before her eyes just then—enveloped in each other's arms, heedless of all.

"Gid-Gideon!" she managed to exclaim at length, more alarmed than shocked, lest the Earl appear of a sudden and discover all.

But even as she called out, a strange choking sound from behind warned her that it was already too late. At the unexpected sound of a human voice the guilty pair sprang apart as if struck by lightning—and at sight of her fiancé Rosalind felt genuinely about to faint, realising instantly what the dire consequences would be.

Meanwhile, the Earl stood goggling, foaming at the mouth like a mad dog—and looking every whit as ferocious, battling with a savage desire to hurl himself at the two and rend them limb from limb. Everyone else suffered varying degrees of embarrassment—except his Grace, who, to his aunt's further astonishment, had recaptured his customary nonchalance and seemed ready to assume command of the situation. Even his sickly look had miraculously vanished, transforming him into his handsome debonair self, as if a burden of great magnitude had been suddenly hoisted from his shoulders.

As his aunt and ward seemed reluctant to speak—and his lordship would find it a sheer impossibility for some time yet—he opened the conversation.

"Methinks an explanation is called for, and—er—some kind of apology," he observed, bluntly.

"A-Ap . . . apology—" spluttered the Earl, with difficulty.

"My dear fellow—do take care," urged the Duke, more concerned about a speck of dust adhering to the bejewelled cuff of his cherry brocade coat. "Can't have you expiring on your wedding eve—"

"How—how dare you, sirrah!" exploded Lord Alnstone, eventually, whipping forth his sword to show he meant action. "Arm yourself, you dirty blackguard, or I'll spit you where you stand!"

"No!" shrieked Rosalind, throwing herself in front of the Duke, whilst the Countess stood wringing her hands helplessly, debating whether to seek help or stay to keep an eye on the situation.

"Faith, 'twould seem your manners ha' gone a-begging, Alnstone, along with your wits," admonished the Duke, "—provoking a hacking-match in front of ladies!"

The Earl—realising his *faux pas* and not wanting to lose face—turned furiously upon Rosalind.

"So!" he bellowed at her. "This is the mysterious cause o' y'r megrims! By Gad! I'll soon cure you once we're wed, rest upon it! Stand aside, trollop! I'll deal with you later."

"Curb your tongue, Alnstone," cautioned the Duke, a sudden edge to his voice. "You grow offensive."

"O-Off-offensive? Me?" screeched his lordship, goaded beyond endurance. "Damme! Y'r audacity is not to be borne, Delvray! Come out from behind her petticoats and I'll show ye just how offensive I can be!" Regardless of the females present, he prepared himself to do battle, sword threateningly poised. "You philanderer! Y-You vile deceiver! You—you wolf in—in—pigskin!"

"Er—sheepskin," corrected his adversary, with infuriating condescension, ushering Rosalind into the comforting arms of his aunt—when to the ladies' relief (and the Earl's annoyance) one or two heads appeared over the shrubbery, with faces in varying stages of astonishment, horror and curiosity, soon to be joined by several more, including Isabella with her newly affianced Viscount, and Sir Roger.

As the crowd gradually swelled—deeming the entertainment outside more diverting than that inside—the Earl's bravado diminished. Though he knew himself to be in the right of it, he also knew the Duke's plausible tongue would soon have the crowd laughing on his side, and himself the butt of his repartee.

"Aunt," breathed Isabella, her brown eyes shuttling back and forth between her brother and the Earl, "what is going on?"

The Countess exchanged meaningful looks with Sir Roger. To anyone but Isabella the situation was blatantly obvious.

"I shall explain later, my dear," whispered her aunt. "Meanwhile, perhaps you would help Sir Roger escort Rosalind up to her room. She looks ready to collapse, poor child." The Countess relinquished Rosalind into her father's tender care, adding as the three made to leave:

"And, Isabella—I forbid any questions."

With that, the Countess and Lord Sevington turned back to witness further developments in the dispute.

"I demand satisfaction!" the Earl was shouting for the tenth time.

The Duke bowed his acknowledgment. "When and where you will, my dear fellow—Viscount Sevington, here, will act for me. You may furnish him with the boring details."

"You will hear the bor—er—you will hear me out, now!" objected Lord Alnstone. "Then you won't be able to concoct any fancy excuses for not presenting yourself. Ten o'clock should be convenient! It shouldn't take above half an hour, which still leaves me ample time to prepare for the ceremony at two."

The Duke regarded him in some amusement. "Your optimism does you credit. You do not anticipate a sudden decline in health?"

"Certainly not—though I cannot guarantee the same for your good self!"

A chuckle of infectious laughter escaped his Grace, but the Earl continued unabashed.

"I suggest we meet in the meadow behind St. Oswald's Churchyard." He paused to indicate a member of the crowd who stepped forward with alacrity and a slight bow. "Darnell, here, will be my second." Then, with a click of heels and a curt bow, he plunged into the crowd to be swallowed up out of sight.

As the guests slowly dispersed, the Viscount excused himself to join Isabella indoors, and the Duke found himself alone in the company of his aunt.

"Well, Gideon?" she challenged, with a wealth of meaning.

"Well, Aunt?" he parried, calmly meeting her look of accusation.

"You realise, of course, that you've been a fool?" she stated rather than questioned, her stout bosom rapidly rising and falling in evidence of the tumult raging within.

"If you say so, Aunt," he agreed, unperturbed.

"A blind stubborn fool! You know as well as I, all this could have been avoided! Forcing the girl along the same ruinous road as her mother! Why, Gideon? Why?"

The Duke flung her a sidelong dubious glance. "I'm afraid I don't quite follow your meaning."

The Countess snorted with annoyance, fidgeting irritably with her fan of painted chicken-skin.

"Surely you do not need me to tell you, Nephew—a man of your experience—what invariably results when a girl pledges her heart to one man and weds another?"

"She naturally overcomes the affliction," he returned naïvely. "Or at least learns to live with it."

"Fiddlesticks!"

He raised an eyebrow in mute enquiry. "Well, Aunt? As you are obviously more widely informed than I, may-hap you would condescend to elucidate. What does result, precisely?"

"A lover!" declared the Countess, with emphasis. "And if she cannot secure the services of the man she loves, then she will end up with a regiment of them, searching in vain for a satisfactory substitute!"

The Duke frowned pensively down at his exquisitely-shod feet. "You—er—think so, Aunt?" he murmured, deep in thought.

"I know so, Gideon," averred her ladyship, adamantly. "I have witnessed it too many times to smack of mere coincidence."

"But by wedding her to someone rich and respectable—"

"Her mother, I hear, began by wedding a man solely for wealth and position," retorted his aunt, turning to follow in the wake of her guests. "And we all know what a disaster that was!"

Having thus given her nephew the benefit of her sound advice, the Countess departed, leaving him to decide whether to act upon it—or not.

15

Rosalind spent the night writhing in suspense, wondering what the morrow would bring. Was she to wed—or not to wed—and if so, whom was she to wed? Furthermore, if it chanced that the Duke came off worst in the tragic duel, how was she to bear the burden for the rest of her days— not only losing him, but knowing she was the direct cause?

Not even Juliet at having to relinquish her Romeo could have suffered greater remorse than she as dawn broke on that sad morn which should have proved the happiest day of her life. Yet, despite this, not long after, she fell into a profound sleep, to be awakened timidly at a quarter to ten by her maid, Betty, bearing her mistress's breakfast tray.

But apparently the short rest had done little to improve her state of mind, or appetite, as she instructed the girl to deposit the tray on the bedside table, grimacing at the coddled eggs, toast and hot chocolate. There, the tray lay ignored whilst she interrogated the maid about the duel, squeezing her dry of any chance piece of gossip she had overheard—most vital of all, when and where it was to take place. But to Rosalind's vexation, the only information Betty had to disclose was nothing she did not already know—that her fiancé had challenged her guardian and they were to fight it out that very morning—the timorous Betty going on to declare that had she known more it would have been her very life's worth to say so, the Countess having forbidden her entire staff to breathe a word of the duel in Miss Rosalind's hearing—and she, being her personal maid, would be first under suspicion.

With a grunt of annoyance, Rosalind sank back into the pillows. She stood greater chance of persuading the King to fling wide the gates of the Fleet, than the Countess to divulge the information she sought! Thus she lay brooding about her unhappy lot, whilst Betty busied herself in the dressing-room in preparation for her mistress's levée—before turning with an air of disrelish to the breakfast again. Deciding to try a morsel, she heaved the tray on to her knees and pushing the eggs aside, found to her astonishment a note tucked underneath. Hastily opening it with fumbling fingers, her eager eyes read written thereon in sprawling characters:

> If you would witness a certain duel to occur within the hour, come at once to the end of the Square—*alone*. A blue coach with yellow wheels will be waiting. *Tell no one!*

Without pausing to think how, when or from whence the note had come, Rosalind leapt out of bed, summoning Betty to help her dress in great speed. Realising she must enlist the aid of someone, she decided to confide in the girl who had been her closest confidante since her arrival at Claremont Park—and who knew how to keep a secret. But at first Betty respectfully protested, begging her mistress not to go, gravely mistrusting the note. However, being much enamoured herself of a certain George Higgins, the third son of a local chandler, she soon gave her support—and even supplied one of her own drab gowns to enable Rosalind to slip out undetected as a serving wench, with a brown shawl to conceal her bright hair, which was sure to betray her. Betty then, under threat of terrible punishment, guided her mistress down the back stairs and out by the servants' entrance, for which Rosalind hugged her gratefully, prevailing upon her to cover up her absence as best she could and not to worry, because she would be back again before noon.

With that, Rosalind crept unobtrusively off down the Square and at the end of the street was delighted to find, sure enough, standing at the corner, an impressive blue coach bearing an unfamiliar coat of arms on the panels, and the wheels picked out in yellow. It obviously belonged to someone of rank, she thought, admiring the four thoroughbreds impatiently pawing the ground, and as the door nearest to her was flung wide invitingly, she ventured inside—surprised to find it completely empty. Furthermore, there were no coachman, postilions, nothing! But no sooner had she disposed herself upon the blue velvet seat than this omission was rectified, for the door slammed, and someone whom she could not see but could certainly hear, clambered up on to the box. Then before she could make a sound the coach gave a violent lurch and was off down the road, rapidly gathering momentum.

Meanwhile, as Rosalind was bowling along the Tyburn Road, spectators were already gathered on St. Oswald's Green, eager to witness what could well prove to be the outstanding event of the year in their calendar, and even laying wagers as to whose gore would be staining the verdant pastures by noon that day, and whether or not any wedding would indeed take place. Tongues wagged continually, elaborating on the wild rumours already in circulation, some averring that the Earl had found the Duke molesting his fiancée—while others pronounced the Duke innocent, having been forced to rescue his ward from her over-amorous husband-to-be.

At two minutes to ten cheers greeted the surgeon, everyone in festive mood, as if about to celebrate the actual wedding instead of someone's execution—and at exactly ten o'clock by St. Oswald's Church, further shouts heralded the arrival of the Earl and his second, Lord Darnell, both clad in sombre grey, as if anticipating a funeral. Grave of visage and dignified of bearing, they advanced across the green to join the small group of officials and patiently await the Duke. But by the time his Grace arrived—fifteen minutes later—their patience was wearing rather thin, and the gathering was quite buoyed up with excitement.

The Duke commanded immediate attention upon his temperamental black stallion, his apricot satin and gold lace afire in the brilliant morning sunlight—with the more quietly but no less fashionably dressed Viscount on his right, while his valet brought up the rear.

The Earl seethed at his adversary's jaunty, almost insolent approach, coupled with his evident popularity with the crowd—but began to smirk to himself at the prospect of the Duke's return, with his lifeless body slung across the stallion's back! See how popular he would be then!

Both flatly repudiated any form of reconciliation, and without further ado prepared themselves for the onslaught, whilst the seconds marked out the area and perused each blade of grass.

When all was ready, the two approached, sword in hand, to be cautioned according to the code, and following the customary salutation, the signal was given and the fight began. A deathly hush descended on the gathering as the two engaged, the Earl decidedly on the attack, bursting with aggression, obviously prepared to hack his rival to pieces in the first six strokes, whilst the Duke languidly parried his every move, as if seeking to win a prize for the least amount of effort.

However, the engagement had not lasted five minutes when an open chaise came tearing up the road to rattle to a standstill by the green—a young girl, elegantly gowned in lemon silk, leaping out before it had time to stop and setting off towards the crowd full tilt, her muslin kerchief fluttering in the breeze, while an elderly gentleman followed in her wake, striving to keep pace with her. On arrival, she continued running round and round the crowd, trying to gain admittance, and on suddenly spying an opening, wriggled her way through to run up breathlessly to the Viscount and shake him vigorously by the arm in desperation for his attention. She was not obliged to shake him long howbeit, for on glancing down to view this audacious person who presumed to lay hands on him, he almost fainted with shock.

"Is-Isabella!" he ejaculated, aghast. "Wh-What on earth are—"

"Rosalind!" gasped out her ladyship. "I-Is she here?"

"R-Rosalind?" queried the stunned Viscount, as if he had never heard the name before.

"She has disappeared! I've come to look for her!"

"Here?"

"Come, Christopher—we must search the crowd! You must help me!" she urged, pulling him towards the throng, adding superfluously as Sir Roger suddenly appeared: "Sir Roger came too!"

The gentlemen exchanged a hasty greeting before Sir Roger embarked upon a breathless account of Rosalind's disappearance according to the confession wrung from her maid ten minutes ago.

"She came to stop the duel," interjected Isabella, as Sir Roger handed Lord Sevington the mysterious note.

"Hum," grunted his lordship, scanning the missive. "If she came at all—I swear, I've seen nought of her. And she could hardly put a stop to it without making her presence known."

"Oh, no!" groaned her ladyship. "I pray Aunt Gertrude isn't right, after all."

"What do you mean?" asked the Viscount, appreciably puzzled.

Sir Roger heaved a sigh, glancing woebegone at his lordship. "The Countess suspects sh-she's b-been . . ." He broke off, unable to voice his worst fears.

"Carried off!" completed Isabella, awestricken.

"Ab-Abducted!" cried Lord Sevington, horrified. "B-But why? How? Who would do such a thing?"

"Lord Alnstone, for one!" supplied his fiancée, flinging a look of accusation at the Earl's back as he continued to battle for an opening in his opponent's guard, oblivious of what was toward behind him.

"Wh-What's to be done?" asked Sir Roger, anxiously.

"I-I'm not quite—hum—sure," stammered his lordship. "I confess it all sounds dash't peculiar."

"You must stop the fight, Christopher!" declared Isabella, dogmatically. "Gideon must be told—he'll know what to do."

But the Viscount cavilled at such a drastic step. If he were to stop the duel and the Duke's ward turned up at home after all—perhaps having just slipped out on some errand—then everyone would claim it a ruse to evade the issue and the Duke branded 'coward' for the rest of his life. It was too risky by far!

However, his very expression was sufficient to tell her ladyship that her husband-to-be was loth to do as she suggested, not appreciating that Rosalind's life could well be at stake—indeed, even being sacrificed at that very moment, whilst they stood dithering, wasting precious time. And so, without a second's thought she took the initiative and plunged headlong between the flashing blades, screaming out for the fight to stop. Fortunately, having kept a furtive eye on her since her arrival, the Duke was half-prepared, and with a sudden swift parry swept the Earl's blade aloft as she dashed beneath it, evoking gasps and screams from the crowd.

Nevertheless, if her sweet head managed to evade the sword, it certainly did not evade her brother's wrath.

" 'Bella!" he roared vehemently, dragging her bodily aside and shaking her till her teeth chattered—whilst the Earl threw down his sword, cursing vociferously to himself, "What the hell do you think you're playing at?"

"B-But it-it's a matter of l-life and d-death," she chattered.

"Yes, you raving maniac—very nearly yours!"

"I-I'm sorry, G-Gideon," she apologised, tearfully.

"Damn it all, girl! I've known you do some scatterbrained things, but—"

"Well, no one else was doing anything, so I had to! Someone had to tell you!"

"Tell me what? It must be devilish important!" he exclaimed, listening with half-interest as he sheathed his sword.

"About Rosalind!"

He hesitated, turning to view her, eyes narrowed, whilst

the Earl, hovering in the background, pricked up his ears at sound of his future wife's name.

"Rosalind?" prompted her brother, curiosity alerted.

"Sh-She's disappeared!"

"She's what?" he demanded, incredulously.

"G-Gone . . . van-vanished . . ." she faltered.

"So, Delvray!" burst in the Earl, rounding on his adversary. "Y'r a deuced coward, to boot! Spiriting her off 'fore the battle's done—frightened I shall win—ha? Ye don't fool me!"

The Duke's suspicious regard came to rest on the Earl in reappraisal of his rival.

"You are either being perfectly honest, Alnstone, or lying confoundedly well—which?"

"Egad! What d'ye mean?" bellowed the other, unsure if he were being complimented or insulted.

"Simply that I know not whether to heed or disregard the doubts about your good self I cherish at present. Many might consider you had more reason than I to resort to such underhanded strategy."

Here, they were joined by the Viscount, overflowing with concern about Isabella's hair-raising intervention—and Sir Roger.

"B-But, Delvray," went on the Earl, feeling uneasy. "If you haven't abducted her, and I haven't—then who the devil has?"

"That, my good fellow, is what I mean to find out if you will but bear with me awhile."

The Duke turned to the Viscount who lost no time in relating the tale, rounding it off by bestowing the note into his charge. As the Duke absorbed the contents a frown descended on his brow which gradually deepened, his lips tightening and expression growing sterner until he finally gave vent to an oath, crushed the paper into a ball and flung it at Lord Alnstone.

"Wh-What is it, Gideon?" stammered the Viscount, voicing the question for everyone, while the Earl smoothed out the note to read it for himself.

"When did this occur?" rasped the Duke.

"I-I believe she left about ten o'clock," supplied Sir Roger, apprehensively. "Almost an hour ago."

"I don't understand," confessed the Earl in puzzled tone. "What does it all mean?"

"It means, my dear Alnstone, that your satisfaction must wait!" snapped his Grace, before curtly demanding his horse.

"Horse?" echoed the Earl in amazement. "S-Surely you aren't going to chase after this blue coach?"

"Can you offer a better suggestion?"

"Dash it, Delvray!" expostulated the Earl, abetted by the rest. "There could be hundreds of blue coaches with yellow wheels!"

The Duke indulged in a cryptic smile. "But one in particular whose owner and I share a mutual aversion, and who would barter his very soul for such an opportunity to settle an old score."

"Gideon!" gasped Lord Sevington. "Y-You can't mean—"

"Chris!" cut in his friend, swiftly. "Take Sir Roger and 'Bella home—there's a good fellow."

This evoked a moan of protest from his sister. "Oh, Gideon! Don't be so mean! Tell us!"

"Come on, Delvray!" supported the Earl, irritably. "If you know something, then speak out! Curse it—me future wife's life is at stake!"

The Duke flung him a look of searing contempt. "Un-

derstand this, Alnstone," he retorted. "I am not obliged
to tell you anything! 'Tis not ten minutes since you considered me a candidate for Bedlam for merely suggesting
what you now seem frantic with impatience to accomplish.
However, because of the grave situation . . ." He broke
off to shrug his shoulders into his coat, proffered by Paul,
and recoup himself for the road, clapping his gold-laced
tricorne on his head as if it were a Breton bonnet.

"Well? Well?" goaded the Earl, exasperated with impatience.

"I nurture a faint suspicion," resumed the Duke, "that
you will find the coach in question less than ten miles out
of London on the Great North Road, bound for Suffolk.
I propose the first to overtake it claims the privilege of
defending the lady's honour."

The Earl gaped at the Duke awhile, then his mouth
clamped shut in a disgruntled line, his suspicions flaring
anew.

"How d'ye know all this?" he challenged. "Why tell me
as much? Who is this mysterious abductor?"

"That, you will discover if—or when—you get there,"
returned the Duke, with strained forbearance.

Here, the Viscount kindly offered Lord Alnstone the use
of his horse, he intending to ride along with his fiancée to
Cavendish Square—for which courteous gesture he was
repaid with a scowl and grumbled acknowledgment before
the Earl again turned on the Duke, convinced he was
being outsmarted.

"I don't believe ye, Delvray—rot me if I do!" he spluttered angrily. " 'S Blood—if 'tis not some infernal ruse to
get me out o' the way on a wild goose chase, so that you
can have her all to y'rself!"

The Viscount winced, wondering how much of the

Earl's petulant provocation his friend was prepared to tolerate, when the Duke's long sufferance finally gave out.

"May the devil eternally plague your soul, Alnstone, the way you've plagued mine this day!" he exploded. "By the Faith! for a man in frenzied desperation to save his damsel in distress, you certainly waste a deal of valuable time in meaningless speculation—apart from overlooking the fact that I've had your future wife to myself for the past twelve months without the need for such contrivance!" —adding as he turned to mount his horse: "Now take yourself off! I've given you enough information to do what is necessary—which is all you're dash't-well going to get!"

But on glancing round again, the Duke found the Earl already half-way across the green to the Viscount's worthy steed, determined to gain a head start on his rival, snatching up his discarded garments ere he leapt into the saddle and off, donning hat and coat as he went.

Strangely, this appeared to afford the Duke amusement, as he reclined against his horse idly contemplating the Earl's rapidly retreating figure.

"Gideon!" urged his lordship, concerned yet puzzled by his friend's reaction. "Make haste! He'll get there before you."

"Aye—verily he will, Chris," murmured the other, pensively. "Verily he will. . . ."

"I-It doesn't bother you?"

"Not unduly."

"B-But I thought you intended saving her yourself?" he remonstrated, confused and irritated by the Duke's ambiguous manner.

"Ah! Now that's another matter . . ." he responded deviously, flashing the Viscount a glance charged with meaning—which seemed to be all he was going to say on the subject.

The Viscount gazed down at the ground, stubbing a divot with his toe as he nervously cleared his throat.

"You—er—appreciate, Gideon, you may have sent him to his—hum—doom?"

"You would rather it were mine?"

"Gideon! I protest! I meant simply—"

"On the contrary, my dear fellow," intersected the Duke, affably. "He galloped off of his own volition—there are witnesses to prove it."

"But it's suicide! He's no match for Romaine!"

Unhurriedly, the Duke mounted his horse aided by his valet, and settled himself comfortably.

"Alas—we all must needs learn the hard way, Chris. Alnstone cannot expect to go through life with a guardian angel at his beck and call—besides, I have too much at stake to waste time playing nursemaid to an unbroken colt who scatters challenges abroad like breadcrumbs, merely for the prestige on't." He adjusted his hat a trifle to the right with painstaking precision, then took up the reins. "Of course, he may well have chosen the lesser of the evils—you forget, he would otherwise have fought me."

The Duke urged his horse into action. "Well, adieu, dear friend." He smiled disarmingly down at the perplexed Viscount. "I trust you will spare me a little of your sympathy . . . I might end up fighting 'em both."

And with a final wave, he trotted off across the meadow.

16

The Duke cantered on his way so light of heart that he unconsciously began to whistle a tuneful air—something he had not done since boyhood—unable to see why the plan already formulated in his mind should go amiss. Not wishing to make his entrance before the opportune moment, he stopped awhile at an inn to refresh himself and make discreet enquiries about the blue coach, but the innkeeper knew nothing.

No whit discouraged, his Grace continued on to repeat the question at every inn he passed, and eventually met with a modicum of success at the fourth. Here, a certain ostler—his memory stimulated by jingling guineas—recalled the coach which, he respectfully informed the Duke, 'tore by at a spankin' pace, with a lunatic on the box—a giant of a man, some ten foot tall and just as wide!'—adding that 'Yer Honour is the second 'igh-flyin' cove to ask about it in the last 'alf-hour.'

So, the boy was rewarded and the Duke resumed his journey, jogging along at the same steady pace, appreciating for the first time in his life the beauty of the countryside on a pleasant October day, smiling up at his feathered friends in acknowledgment of their cheery song —instead of consigning them to the devil as was his wont —and even dumbfounding a group of farm labourers in the fields by politely doffing his hat to them in greeting.

On he travelled, rapt in admiration of Mother Nature— to suddenly pull up short and listen intently. Sure enough, was borne to his ear on the gentle breeze the faint ring and clash of steel—he judged about a hundred yards or so round the next bend. Urging his horse over the grass and through the hedge into the field beyond, he dismounted and tethered it out of sight, then crept furtively along behind the hedgerow in the direction of the sound. The sound of fencing grew louder—evidence that the duel he had anticipated was well under way—and when reasonably near he peered cautiously over the hedge to see the coach —the door swung ajar—stationary by the roadside, whilst Sir Francis and Lord Alnstone attacked each other with gusto a little to the left—apparently enjoying it!

Keeping stealthily out of sight, the Duke crept even nearer, and when close enough to the coach looked inside —but for the second time that day, the vehicle stood empty. This evoked the inevitable curse from him. Obviously, being the resourceful female she was, his ward had already seized her chance of escape.

As she was nowhere in the immediate vicinity, he retreated from the scene of battle as unobtrusively as he had approached, and remounting his horse, sat awhile straining his eyes over the surrounding area—but of Rosalind there was no sign. Presumably she had made her escape on the Earl's arrival—reasoned the Duke—therefore could not have travelled far hence afoot—but which way?

Not having encountered her along the road, he set off to scour the countryside, and when a safe distance from his rivals, broke into a fast gallop, with eyes constantly on the alert.

He had not travelled more than a mile when he spied what appeared to be an old peasant woman stooped almost double, seemingly resting on the brow of a hill as if the strenuous climb was too much for her aged limbs. Intending to enquire of her if she had seen ought of the female he sought, the Duke at once steered his horse towards her—but on hearing the hoofbeats, without as much as a glance at the rider, she promptly set off uphill in peculiar lolloping bounds like an overgrown bird with its wings clipped—to the Duke's wide-eyed astonishment.

"Stop!" he called out—which seemed to make her the more determined not to, injecting renewed vigour into her tired legs as she hopped briskly over the summit and off down the other side with the Duke hot on her tail. He reached the top in time to see her lose balance and catapult head-over-heels to the bottom in a flurry of white petticoats and pink bestockinged legs (much too shapely for any peasant woman)—to land with a thump, a dishevelled bundle of grey homespun and long tangled yellow hair.

A chuckle erupted from the Duke as he cantered on down the hill and dismounted beside her—but Rosalind, despite being blinded by hair and bound head and foot, was already making a valiant effort to rise, which presented something of a problem. A kerchief had gagged her mouth, but this now hung suspended round her neck. With much contorting and straining, puffing and panting, she struggled to her knees—only to be pushed down again by her guardian who knelt to untie her bonds. Nevertheless, for this service one may have expected her to repay him with a modicum of gratitude, but instead she began to hurl abuse at his head and wrestled violently on the grass, determined to make his task the harder.

"Leave me alone, you beast!" she spat at him. "Y-You cut-throat! Murderer! If you touch me I'll scream—loud enough to deafen everyone in London!" Puff—pant. "I

wouldn't marry you if you were the only man breathing—
or if you offered me the Crown Jewels—or if you were the
King himself!" Puff—pant. "I wouldn't marry you"—gasp
—"even if you hadn't killed the man I loved . . ."—this
somewhat tearfully, then furiously: "I hate you! I hate
you! D'you hear me? I *hate* you!"

" 'Pon my soul—what an inconstant female you are, to
be sure," observed the Duke, when given a chance. "I'll
warrant your moods are even more capricious than our
intemperate clime."

Her struggling ceased abruptly and she lay perfectly
still, wondering if she had heard aright. Then suddenly
appreciating her freedom, she sat bolt upright, sweeping
hair aside to stare spellbound at her guardian for some
time, paralysed, speechless—while the Duke regarded her
in growing uneasiness.

"Rosalind?" he probed apprehensively. "Child—are you
all right?" His eyes swept over her unable to see ought
amiss.

"Y-You are al-alive . . ." she breathed, as if witnessing
a miracle.

"Of course I'm alive!" he laughed in surprise. "Pray,
why shouldn't I be?"

But instead of seeing the humorous side—to the Duke's
disconcertion—she threw herself into his arms and burst
into tears.

" 'Od's Life, child!" he protested lightheartedly. "If you
aren't drenching me in tea, I'll wager it's tears."

"B-But I thought y-you . . . w-were . . . d-dead," she
blubbered into his coat. "I-I thought h-he'd . . . k-killed
. . . y-you."

"By the saints! 'Twill take more than some pompous
loud-mouthed braggart to dispatch me to my Maker!

Come, come—weeping on your wedding day? That's the 'groom's privilege."

But the very mention of the word 'wedding' evoked a veritable cloudburst—which wrought a sudden change in the Duke, who swept aside his levity to reveal an earnest tenderness beneath.

"Please don't cry, Rosalind," he besought her in a whisper. "You've been a real trump so far—don't fall apart now with the winning-post in sight."

"W-Winning-p-post?" she sobbed.

"You've won, child—routed the enemy—as you vowed you'd do in Vauxhall Gardens—remember? You have achieved the impossible . . . and brought Daring Delvray to his knees within three months."

"I-I have?" she faltered timidly, striving to meet his gaze as he untied the kerchief swathing her neck and raised up her face to dry her eyes, whilst he continued unburdening his heart.

"I am ready to admit defeat, Rosalind—ready to admit I love you, worship you, with my heart and soul—confess to being several kinds of fool—and that I've been driven to distraction with a damnable heartache over the past months—and would have died a thousand agonising deaths if you'd married Alnstone. . . ."

As he breathed his final words his lips were on hers, in a kiss of torrid passion, his arms crushing her to him, and with a groan of sheer ecstasy Rosalind surrendered herself to the overpowering desire consuming her, as she dissolved in the intense heat of his blazing ardour, thrilling wildly in the knowledge that his need for her was as great as hers for him.

"How I've loved you!" he gasped at length. "Ever since you lay in my arms, my Rosalind, the sun of my life—

lying pale and deathly with your life's blood dripping on the floor—my soul has been in constant torment! Never have I wanted to sacrifice my life for anyone before, or felt so useless! What I would have given to have changed places with you—to have borne your suffering . . . the agony was crucifying, knowing I was to blame . . . repeatedly cursing myself for not finishing the job when I had my two hands round her throat. . . ." He stopped, shaking off his momentary madness, to resume choked with feeling. "Rosalind, my dearest life, you overwhelm me with pride, but also a deep humiliation at my own shortcomings . . . the way I have used you so shamefully! I pray in all sincerity, that one day you will perhaps find it in your loving, generous heart to forgive me . . . and forget."

But Rosalind was in no state of mind to forgive anyone anything. The blood swirled round her brain like a flaming whirlpool as his lips scorched her face, neck—driving her to the verge of madness—which he must have sensed, to suddenly put her from him.

"Come, child—this won't do at all!" he breathed, wiping a hand across his forehead. "We must be gone!"

"G-Gone? Wh-Where?" she stammered stupidly, still labouring beneath the effects of his hypnotic passion as he rose to his feet.

The Duke dusted himself down, straightened his hat, then gallantly assisted her also to rise.

"My dear young lady, have you forgotten that in little over an hour a church full of illustrious guests will be assembled to witness a marriage—your marriage?"

"Marriage!" she ejaculated, awaking with a jolt to reality, her clouded brain struggling to establish precisely what he had in mind—conscious of the fact that although he had mentioned marriage, had yet again carefully avoided any reference to his own. Was it possible he still expected her to wed the Earl?

Whilst the Duke retrieved his horse, she calmly stood by, intending to draw his attention to the oversight.

"It would seem your noble guests are destined for a long wait, my Lord Duke," she remarked, pleasantly, on his return, slyly surveying him through her lashes.

"Why?" he replied innocently, adjusting the saddle-girth. "Surely you can be ready in an hour?"

"I can—but what of the bridegroom?"

"Bridegroom? Why should he take any longer to prepare himself?"

"Because first of all, your Grace, we must needs find one."

The unfortunate animal emitted a sharp whinny of protest as the saddle-girth was wrenched a little too tightly —evidence that her point had registered. The Duke completed his task, then stood up, the personification of guilt.

"Ah—er—bridegroom . . . y-yes . . . hm . . . mm . . ." His eyes flitted from tree to tree, flower to flower, swept up aloft to survey the blue skies, then down to examine the grass at his feet. "Er—mayhap we could rectify the matter," he ventured anon—more to himself.

Rosalind maintained a prudent silence as he took the horse by the rein and her by the arm, to stroll through the pleasant glade.

" 'Twould be a pity to disappoint such noble gathering, would it not?" he observed—still avoiding her gaze.

"A great pity, your Grace," she responded, tongue in cheek.

"Not to mention the shocking waste of such lavish banquet which has set me back to the tune of some fifty thousand—and which my aunt has expended prodigious time and energy arranging?"

"Quite so, your Grace."

"And as it's being held in my own house . . . I-I don't . . . sup . . . pose . . ."

"Yes?" she prompted eagerly, despite herself.

"Yes?"—he cast her a downward look of censure.

"Oh—er—y-your Grace," she appended, straight-faced.

"That's better! Now let me see . . . where was I?"

"You weren't supposing," supplied Rosalind, coyly.

"Ah—yes!" he resumed, his arm progressing to her shoulders. "I—er—wasn't supposing you might consider" —cough—"exchanging an Earl . . . for a hm . . . mm . . . Duke?" Having finally managed to utter the words he heaved a sigh, appreciating for the first time precisely why the Viscount 'hummed' so frequently.

"I'm afraid I don't quite know what you mean, your Grace."

The Duke pulled up short, jerking his arm away. "Plague take ye, woman! Ye know damned well what I mean!"

"Having misconstrued your meaning once before, my Lord Duke—to my bitter disillusionment," replied she, infuriatingly composed, "alas, I must insist you make your request more explicit."

This quelled his outburst like magic, and he threw her a sheepish glance—like a small boy caught raiding his mother's larder.

"Very well," he smiled whimsically, doffing his hat to sweep her a flourishing bow. "Miss Tremayne, would you deign to wed me—become my wife—my Duchess—accept me in place of yon cut-and-thrust Alnstone? . . . Is that explicit enough, Mistress?"

"Yes, your Grace," she replied, eyes demurely lowered.

He cast her a look loaded with suspicion. "And what exactly does that mean—yes, it's explicit—or yes, you consent?"

"Yes, it's explicit," she answered, meekly.

The Duke swore beneath his breath, and seizing her by the shoulders dragged her round to face him.

"Confound you, minx! Do you accept or not?"

Rosalind dimpled up at him, coquettishly. "You really wish to wed me, Gideon?"

" 'Pon rep! If 'tis the only way to put an end to this 'your Gracing' and 'Lord Duking' me at every breath—'s Death!—what choice do I have?"

"You are absolutely sure? No thimble-rigging this time?"

The Duke coughed, sniffed, but managed to preserve his countenance as he assured her his offer was profoundly sincere.

"In which case, I accept most willingly."

"You—er—wouldn't care to ponder on't awhile?" he volunteered obligingly. "I should be loth to accept a hasty decision."

Rosalind shook her head vigorously.

"Then if you are perfectly certain, Miss Tremayne," he went on, drawing her gradually back into his arms, "may I be allowed to seal the agreement in the conventional way?"

"If you wish, my Lor—"

"Don't you dare!" he warned, before his lips smothered the rest of her words.

"Gideon?" she breathed anxiously, at length. "Won't Lord Alnstone be furious when he finds out how you've tricked him—and-and perhaps challenge you to another duel?"

The Duke chuckled. "Belike he won't be much amused —or in any fit state to do much about it either, when our friend Romaine's done with him."

He had led her up to the horse and was about to assist her into the saddle when he hesitated, viewing her strangely.

"Y-Yes, Gideon?" she prompted gently, sensing something grave.

"My—er—past in no wise troubles you?" he queried dubiously, as if it apparently troubled him.

"You mean your wicked reputation?" she supplied naïvely—making him flinch. "When you first brought me to Claremont Park, I must own it did—but I soon realised how terribly wrong I was to prejudge you so. Not only did you take me into your home and lavish everything on me, but placed the world at my feet and treated me like a lady, with honour and respect which, at the time, I certainly did not deserve! Your conduct towards me—under the circumstances, Gideon—has been above censure at all times, and to me you are the most wonderful—".

"Damn it, Rosalind! Don't make me out to be the saint I'm not!" he thundered, almost throwing her on to the horse in his resentment. "Heaven knows I was bad enough before—but the night Dame Fortune dropped you into my lap all the diabolical fiends of hell were unleashed inside me at sight of you standing there, knee-deep in your misery and despair! I took you into my house, fed you, clothed you—yes, even launched you into Society—not because it was Good Samaritan Week, but because I realised in you the fulfilment of my life's ambition—"

"Revenge on my mother?"

"However, my love, what you do not appreciate is—had my revenge on your mother proved fruitless, I intended wreaking the entire wrath of it on your innocent head, merely because you resembled her, for want of a better reason!"

"But you didn't, did you, Gideon?" she countered calmly.

He stood awhile eyeing her in sullen discontent, as if almost wishing he had.

"No," he grudged, hurrying on, determined to paint his character as black as possible. "Even so, you must see, Rosalind, everything I did on your behalf was done with the most ulterior of motives? I didn't suffer a single pang of conscience at the likelihood of you being ruined, harmed—even killed!"

The fact that she remained utterly self-possessed served only to exasperate him further.

"Rosalind!" he bellowed up at her, goaded beyond endurance. "Haven't you understood a single word I've said?"

"My Lord Duke," she responded unmoved, gazing serenely down on him. "I was well aware of the risk involved and the role you had destined for me long before we journeyed to London for my presentation—furthermore, had already accepted it. I never expected a man of your repute and distinction to so inconvenience himself on my behalf without gaining something. I did not know precisely what, until my father hinted that you had been more than friendly with my mother. After that, it was a simple enough task to fill in the blank spaces."

The Duke stared aghast. "Y-You didn't mind being used thus?"

"Why should I? What would my life have been otherwise, when the gallows loomed on the horizon? Besides, I haven't come out of it so badly."

"Nevertheless, your past year has been anything but smooth!"

"You can't be held wholly responsible for that, Gideon," she corrected gently. "You must agree, most of my misfortunes were brought about by my own reckless behaviour. At Vauxhall, had I not wandered off alone, I shouldn't have suffered the degradation I did—and if I had heeded your commands to quit the drawing-room during my mother's visit I doubt if I should have finished up shot in the head! Even this ultimate abduction by Sir Francis would not have happened had I not acted irresponsibly and sneaked out without your aunt's knowledge —though I feel she may have done the same when she was young—to save the life of the man she loved, as I believed I was doing."

The Duke felt obliged to agree and capitulated with a sigh as he finally swung himself up behind, encircling her waist with his arms as he took up the reins.

"You're a stubborn minx!" he lightly admonished her. "You can see me as nought else but your infernal knight in shining armour! A pox on't! Ye've stuck me on a plaguey pedestal on which I'll have a devilish time keepin' me balance!"

"Despair not, my love," she consoled him. "Your Duchess will always be on hand to save you when you fall—and if you are extra good"—she smiled up at him mischievously—"you may even be afforded the luxury of attending my ablutions."

"Permit me to correct you, my angel," he returned swiftly, a wicked gleam in his eye. "I shall attend regularly whether I am good, bad—or as fiendish as Lucifer!"